The PARIS Project

Also by Donna Gephart

In Your Shoes

Lily and Dunkin

Death by Toilet Paper

How to Survive Middle School

Olivia Bean, Trivia Queen

As If Being 12¾ Isn't Bad Enough,
My Mother Is Running for President!

The PARIS Project

DONNA GEPHART

Simon & Schuster Books for Young Readers

NEW YORK   LONDON   TORONTO   SYDNEY   NEW DELHI

SIMON & SCHUSTER BOOKS FOR YOUNG READERS
An imprint of Simon & Schuster Children's Publishing Division
1230 Avenue of the Americas, New York, New York 10020
SIMON & SCHUSTER BOOKS FOR YOUNG READERS
is a trademark of Simon & Schuster, Inc.
For information about special discounts for bulk purchases, please contact
Simon & Schuster Special Sales at 1-866-506-1949 or business@simonandschuster.com.
The Simon & Schuster Speakers Bureau can bring authors to your live event.
For more information or to book an event, contact the Simon & Schuster Speakers
Bureau at 1-866-248-3049 or visit our website at www.simonspeakers.com.
Jacket design by Lizzy Bromley
Interior design by Hilary Zarycky
The text for this book was set in New Baskerville.
Manufactured in the United States of America
0819 FFG
First Edition
2 4 6 8 10 9 7 5 3 1
Library of Congress Cataloging-in-Publication Data
Names: Gephart, Donna, author.
Title: The Paris Project / Donna Gephart.
Description: First edition. | New York : Simon & Schuster Books for Young Readers,
[2019] | Summary: Cleveland Rosebud Potts yearns to leave Sassafras, Florida for a rich and cultured life at The American School of Paris, but problems with family, friends, and finances stand in her way.
Identifiers: LCCN 2018055764 | ISBN 9781534440869 (hardcover : alk. paper)
| ISBN 9781534440883 (ebook)
Subjects: | CYAC: Self-actualization—Fiction. | Family life—Florida—Fiction. | Prisoners' families—Fiction. | Friendship—Fiction. | Florida—Fiction.
Classification: LCC PZ7.G293463 Par 2019 | DDC [Fic]—dc23
LC record available at https://lccn.loc.gov/2018055764

*To those who strive toward social justice with a helpful,
hopeful heart and an open, optimistic mind.
And to you, dear reader. When you feel alone or lost, may a
book be your trusted friend, a connection to grace, and an
emotional road map that leads you home.*

An older sister is a friend and defender—
a listener, conspirator, a counselor and a sharer of delights.
And sorrows too.

—PAM BROWN

The PARIS Project

A Bad Beginning

ONDAY I GOT KICKED OUT of ballet school.

Not just a class, mind you. Apparently, what I did was bad enough to get me banned from the entire school for the rest of my life.

Maybe I should have listened to Miss Delilah, the school's owner, when my sister, Georgia, signed me up at the beginning of August, three weeks before school began.

"Cleveland, dear." Miss Delilah stared at me over the frames of her eyeglasses. "You should start in the beginner class, since you don't have other dance experience."

I didn't tell Miss Delilah how Georgia and I used to dance like no one was watching. (Until we discovered the creepy neighbor boy, Jacob Andrews, was actually watching. He peeked at us through the window of our trailer because he had a big, heart-busting crush on Georgia. Luckily for us, Jacob and his family moved to a remote Alaskan island for his mom's job as a geologist, where the only things he'd be spying on were snow, melting ice, and polar bears, which was really good news unless you were a polar bear who liked its privacy.)

I also didn't tell Miss Delilah there was no way—*pas question*—I'd go into a class filled with babies who picked their noses and fell over sideways when they tried to stand in third position. I had learned about ballet positions, posture, poise, and other important things online, so I'd be prepared to enter the advanced class for girls my age. I'd been practicing in front of the mirror in our bedroom.

Tugging on the sides of my red beret, I kept my back pencil straight, like I figured French girls were trained to do when talking to the heads of their dance schools. "If you don't mind, I'd rather take a class with girls my age."

Miss Delilah contorted her face in a very unflattering way, as though she were trying to hold in a toot. "Cleveland, I'm sure you're very talented, but it's my professional opinion—"

"If Cleveland wants to be with girls her age," Georgia interjected, "that's where she should be." Then my sister opened her I ♥ VERMONT wallet, which she bought because she planned to attend the University of Vermont the following year, and she pulled out a bunch of twenty-dollar bills that I knew came from her job cashiering at Weezie's Market and Flower Emporium.

Georgia had to scan a lot of cans of creamed corn to earn that much cash. I would've had the money to pay for the class myself if only . . .

"Here's the fee for the *advanced* class," Georgia said.

I felt like a balloon filled almost to bursting. *Thank you, Georgia!*

"Okay, Cleveland," Miss Delilah said. "Let's head over to the studio and see what you already know."

Georgia and I followed her to a room with a mirrored wall and a barre along the opposite wall. It felt so official that I got twelve kinds of tingly.

I stood in the middle of the dance floor while Georgia hung back by the door, her arms crossed, like she was daring Miss Delilah to say one mean thing to me. Everyone should have a big sister like Georgia. She's protected me like the secret service since I was in kindergarten and Joey Switzer put a worm down my shirt. Let's just say that boy hasn't even looked at me sideways since Georgia, who was in fifth grade at the time, had a little chat with him at recess. We Potts girls stick together and look out for each other like that.

Miss Delilah held on to the barre and faced me. Her posture was stick-straight like the women in the videos. "Demonstrate first position, please."

I held myself tall and turned my feet out in my best first position, wishing I were wearing ballet slippers instead of my ratty old sneakers, with holes forming near the pinkie toes. I hoped Miss Delilah didn't notice.

She didn't seem bothered by my sneakers. "Fine. Second position, please."

I moved my legs apart and held my arms out, like they were delicate feathers about to float down to my sides.

"Third position."

This one was tougher, because I don't think feet are meant to turn so far in the opposite direction, but I did it and forced myself to smile like I saw a ballerina do in a book called *Ballet for Beginners*. I'd be able to do a better job when I was wearing a leotard and tights instead of shorts and a T-shirt, but I guessed I was doing all right because I peeked up at Georgia, and she nodded. I could tell from how happy she looked that she was proud of me.

That filled me up, squeezed out the nervousness.

"Let's head back to my office now, girls."

Georgia and I sat on the same chairs in front of Miss Delilah's desk as when we first came in.

"Well then." Miss Delilah lowered herself into her seat and folded her hands. "I suppose we could put Cleveland in the class with girls her age. At least she'll be starting at the beginning of the year with everyone else. Classes start the same day school begins." Miss Delilah removed her eyeglasses and let them hang on a beaded chain around her neck, then rubbed the bridge of her nose, like she was trying to relieve a headache. "Even if Cleveland's willing to work diligently, I still don't think advanced ballet is the best—"

"Thanks so much," Georgia said, cutting her off before she could say something my sister didn't want to hear.

"Yeah, thanks," I offered. Joy bubbled inside me because I had the forethought to learn the ballet positions online so I didn't look like an *imbécile* in front of Miss Delilah when she tested me. It felt like when a teacher gave a surprise quiz in school and I knew all the answers.

"The permission form and contract require a parent's signature," Miss Delilah said.

5

Georgia pulled out the forms Mom had signed last night. "We printed them from your website."

What my sister didn't say was we printed the forms at the Sassafras Public Library on Main Street and Third Avenue, because we didn't have a printer at home, and we had only Georgia's old laptop, which Mom and I borrowed when we needed to.

"All righty then."

When Miss Delilah got up to file the forms in a cabinet, Georgia flashed me a thumbs-up and winked.

I tried to wink back, but both eyes closed at the same time. I stunk at winking. It didn't matter. I was going to be a ballerina! I imagined myself wearing a black leotard and pink tights and spinning, spinning like the ballerinas I watched and read about. I wondered if there would be any boys in the class whose job it would be to throw us into the air. That might be fun, as long as they didn't drop us because we weighed too much for their scrawny muscles. Maybe we could toss the boys into the air instead. The thought made me giggle, so I covered my mouth.

Miss Delilah's lips moved as she silently counted my sister's cash. "The class costs a hundred dollars, plus the registration fee for new students. You owe me twenty more dollars." She held out her palm, fingers spread.

Georgia dug into her wallet and plucked out one more crumpled bill, which she dropped into Miss Delilah's hand.

I'm sorry, I wanted to say. It wasn't my fault I didn't have the money to pay for the class myself. A bolt of anger sizzled through me. Then guilt stabbed at my stomach for feeling angry. I knew things were hard for Dad right now, so I felt uncomfortable every time I got angry with him. But really, things were difficult for all of us because of what he'd done. And that made me angry all over again. I let out a slow breath, hoping the anger would leak out with it.

The corners of Miss Delilah's mouth rose slightly. "Cleveland, we look forward to your joining our little family here at Miss Delilah's School of Dance and Fine Pottery."

Even though I already had a family and didn't want to be part of Miss Delilah's, a tingle zinged along my spine. I felt better. The first item on my Paris Project list was about to be accomplished and checked off. Only five more items to go, and then I'd be on my way to Paris, France. I could practically smell the warm, buttery croissant I'd nibble as I strolled past the Eiffel Tower, breathing in all that refreshing Paris air. Everything about going to school and living in Paris would be a thousand times better than doing those things here in Sassafras, Florida, where people could be downright nasty for no good reason. Plus, it wouldn't be so blasted hot in Paris. I checked. In Sassafras in August, it's a disgusting average eighty-two degrees of pure humidity. The average August temperature in Paris is seventy-five degrees of pure perfection. I couldn't wait.

Life in Paris would be *magnifique*!

Things were finally going like they were supposed to.

Until Jenna Finch and her stupid pinkie toe had to go and ruin everything.

Oh la la la la! (Which, for your information, actually means "Oh no no no no!")

The Truth about What Happened to the Paris Project Money

MY FASCINATION/OBSESSION WITH PARIS, FRANCE, started when I was little and Mom read me the Madeline picture books from the library. I'm looking at you, Miss Clavel. I could tell how much Mom wished she could travel to Paris by the way she pointed out each landmark—the Eiffel Tower, Notre-Dame, the Luxembourg Gardens—and then looked into the distance and let out a slow sigh, like she was imagining herself there. It made me want to visit them too.

When I was in fourth and fifth grade, I'd pore over Mom's travel magazines and books, focusing on everything I could find about Paris. I even discovered an old book from one of the library book sales in the back of a kitchen drawer. It had black-and-white aerial photos of the entire city. I'd examine the photos and let out a long, slow sigh like Mom used to when she read *Madeline*. "I'd sure love to get to Paris someday," I'd tell her.

Mom would nod, her dark, curly hair bobbing. "Doesn't cost anything to dream, Cleveland. I've been doing it all my life."

I didn't want to only dream about going to Paris. I needed to figure out a way to get there, especially after starting Sassafras Middle School last year. Elementary school was great, so I'd thought middle school would be more of the same. Nope!

From the first day of sixth grade, Jenna Finch decided not to be friends with me anymore. And I don't even know what I did wrong, other than keep living at Sunny Smiles Trailer Park with the faded happy face on the sign at the entrance, while Jenna and her family moved from two trailers down to a big house on the hill the summer before middle school started. It wasn't even like they earned that big house. Everyone knew they got it because Jenna's granny won a ton of money in a lawsuit when she got hit by a bus and ended up in a wheelchair. I was sorry for what happened to her granny, but moving to that house changed Jenna. She stopped talking to me. Whenever I asked about hanging out, she was busy. When we finally got to middle school, where I needed her more than ever, she chose to hang out with the rich girls and pretended I was 100 percent invisible.

Sometimes I wondered if I was.

It hurt eating lunch by myself in a new school and watching my former friend talking and laughing with a bunch of other girls. And my other good friend, Declan Maguire, had another lunch period, since he was a grade older than me. Sitting alone did give me plenty of time to hatch my plan. That was when I decided the only solution was getting away from Sassafras Middle School. Far, far away: 4,498 miles (7,239 kilometers), to be exact. That's the distance between Sassafras and Paris. I checked.

I created a real plan—the Paris Project—that involved the American School of Paris and me getting a scholarship so I could attend. There were a bunch of other things I'd need to do, but if I followed each step of the plan, I knew I'd make it happen.

When I earned that scholarship and enough money to move to Paris, I'd find a way to pay for Mom to visit me there. Together, we'd explore the famous art museum the Louvre, and smile at *Mona Lisa* or stick out our tongues, depending on what kind of mood we were in. Then, when we got tired of looking at all that great art, we'd find an outdoor café and eat French pastries and drink cups of *café au lait*, pointing our pinkie fingers out while we drank. Mom deserved a fun, fancy vacation like that. And we'd have no problem finding a place to do that, because there are approximately seven thousand cafés in Paris, unlike in Sassafras, where there are approximately zero, unless you count the outdoor tables at the McDonald's on Route 40.

Taking ballet lessons (to acquire some culture) was the first item on my Paris Project list. Before I could start ballet class, though, Miss Delilah let me know I needed to purchase certain required items, which she conveniently sold behind a counter at her school.

So I walked through the blazing August heat to Miss Delilah's the day after Georgia signed me up, and picked out a pair of pink tights, a black leotard, and ballet shoes in size ten. Georgia and I inherited our dad's huge feet. He wore size twelve, which is like a woman's thirteen and a half. She wore size eleven. *Tellement gros!* So big! I also got Dad's whisper-fine blond hair, but Georgia inherited Mom's thick, curly black hair. Lucky!

Miss Delilah held out a small box of bobby pins too. "You'll need these, Cleveland, to pin your hair up for class. It looks too short for a bun."

My hair was definitely too short for a bun. It was too short to do anything but sit on my head and be boring, but I didn't want to spend more money than absolutely necessary.

Miss Delilah stood behind the counter with the bobby-pin box in her hand, waiting.

"Okay. Thanks." I put the box onto my pile of ballet clothes. "How much will that be altogether?"

I held my breath while she added it up. There were exactly eighty dollars squished into my pocket, everything I'd been able to save from my dog-walking business after Dad—

Turns out my three customers dropped me like a hot potato after what happened to Dad was written about in the *Sassafras Star Gazette.* Luckily, I got a new customer at the beginning of July when I put up a sign on the bulletin board near the community pool. It was Declan's idea to put up the sign, because I wasn't in the mood to do much of anything then. The people who called me had just moved into our neighborhood and needed someone to walk their dog on weekday afternoons. It was perfect. They hadn't been told yet to worry about trusting anyone from the Potts family with their house key.

Now my hands squeezed into fists so hard my

half-chewed fingernails dug into my palms and made painful half-moons there.

"Fifty-eight dollars and sixty-seven cents," Miss Delilah said. "Unless you want to add an extra pair of tights. Those things sometimes get runs, and you can't wear tights with runs to class."

"I'll be real careful."

"All righty then."

I forced a smile as I handed all that cash to Miss Delilah.

"Thank you, Cleveland." She gave me the change and patted my hand. "See you at our first class in a few weeks."

I took my paper bag and held it to my chest. "See you then."

As I left the dance school and walked past the other stores along the strip mall, even the auto supply store, I felt good, like I belonged to something important—a ballet class—and I had the special clothes in a bag to prove it. I was going to experience culture. I was going to make it to Paris!

But as I walked farther, past the cemetery and the big vacant lot and through the center of town, that good feeling seeped away. It was replaced by a niggling feeling of anger that grew into something jagged inside me. When I passed the diner at Main Street and Second Avenue, a block down from the library, I was convinced the old people eating there were staring at me through the front window and talking about me. About my dad.

What Dad did was big news in our boring town. I wish he could have become famous for doing something good, like creating the world's funniest joke or curing cancer or swimming the English Channel, which is twenty-two miles of water between England and France, instead of what he actually did.

I breathed hard through my nose and stomped forward, clutching my new ballet clothes. Sweat stung my eyes and ran in droplets off the tip of my nose, but I didn't care. I kicked a rock on the sidewalk. It struck a stop-sign pole with a satisfying *clink*.

Deep inside, a scream waited to explode. I'd saved $960 from the dog-walking business that I started last March. Three different customers with one dog walk every afternoon at twenty dollars per week. It was great money, and I loved spending time with the dogs, except for one little yappy guy named Mr. Bossypants. I'd saved almost a thousand dollars! That's a lot of dog walking in the heat and a lot of poop picking up. That's a lot of time and energy.

I'd still have that money for my Paris Project if my dad hadn't gone into my room that Saturday, June 20, when I was at Declan's house, telling him how sad I was about what was going to happen to my dad in exactly ten days. If Dad hadn't pried open my Eiffel Tower tin—the one he'd given me for my eleventh birthday and knew I was using to store my dog-walking money—and stolen every dollar out of it. He was probably surprised by how much was in there, because I hadn't told my parents how much I'd earned. I was thinking of asking if I could open a bank account for the money and wish I'd done that, because now it was gone.

How was I supposed to get out of Sassafras without that money? And staying here had become a thousand times harder with everyone looking at us sideways or away from us, which was even worse.

My breathing came in ragged gasps, and I felt unsteady, like I might topple over, so I sat on a bus bench and put my head in my hands with the paper bag beside me. I practiced the slow breathing Georgia taught me to do when I got upset, but it wasn't working. The memory rushed in.

The tin was empty and lying on my bedroom floor when I came home. At first I thought someone had broken into our trailer and stolen the money, but nothing else was touched. The front door had been locked and no windows were even open.

It didn't take long to find out that Dad had taken my Paris Project money to spend at his favorite place on the planet—the dog-racing park—which wasn't a place for dogs to run and play and have fun. It was a place where grown-ups gambled on dog races and also played poker, according to Mom.

Even though I'd never been there, I hated that place!

It was where Dad was when he should have been home. It was where he started going in January with his old high school friend Mr. Tom, who turned out to be no friend at all. Mom's face always pinched up when she told us Dad was there. I guess Dad went so much that he ran out of his own money to gamble with and decided to start taking other people's.

How could he do something like that?

My dad did that.

My dad, who played in the community pool with me and Georgia, who sang wobbly love songs to our dog, Miss Genevieve, who creamed my corn in Monopoly on a regular basis.

My dad stole all my Paris Project money.

I couldn't imagine ever forgiving him for that . . . and especially for what happened right afterward. I know that wasn't entirely his fault, but still.

• • •

In the sweltering Florida heat, I let out a slow, quavering breath, tugged the red beret tight on my sweaty head, and wrapped my arms around myself.

Why did everything have to be so difficult?

I bet nothing was this *difficile* in Paris!

According to Mom's travel guides and magazines, Paris seemed to be a thousand times better than Sassafras. *Un millier de fois!*

Trying Hard to Be Enough

ON MONDAY, AUGUST 24, AFTER my first day of seventh grade, I planned to arrive at Miss Delilah's School of Dance and Fine Pottery twenty minutes early, because I still had to put on my ballet clothes and didn't want to miss a minute of instruction, especially since Georgia paid so much for my classes.

Sweat pooled under my armpits and dripped down my sides. It was always hot in Sassafras, even during most of the winter. After school I needed to rush home to take care of our pooch, Miss Genevieve, who had all-white fur except for a brown patch around his right eye, and the Mirandas' dog, Scarlett Bananas, who was white with brown patches and two cute floppy brown ears. I gave Miss Genevieve a quick walk, which I didn't get paid for. Then I gave Scarlett Bananas a longer walk, which I would be paid twenty dollars for at the end of the week.

Cleveland's Parisian Dog Walking at your service! (Some of my customers have asked about the name of my company, so I point to my red beret, which is perfectly Parisian. But I don't mention I practice speaking French with my four-legged customers. *Oh, beau chien.* Oh, beautiful dog. My furry friends never correct my pronunciation or make fun of me.)

Scarlett Bananas was my only customer at the moment. I'd been walking her for about eight weeks. It was hard to build my Paris Project fund back up with only one customer and needing to buy clothes for ballet class, but I was doing the best I could. Maybe when I moved to Paris, I'd have more customers. I hoped so, because I'd miss our dog terribly, plus I'd need the money. It is very expensive to live there. *Très cher!*

I grabbed the bag with my *très cher* dance clothes and headed to Declan's. There was still time before I had to leave for dance class, and I knew Declan would help me feel less nervous about my first day.

I hustled along the extended horseshoe-shaped

driveway that ran through our trailer park, past the community pool and car-washing station, along the path to the Maguire trailer. It was easy to spot their trailer because it was covered with bumper stickers, like KEEP CALM AND FIDDLE ON and FIDDLERS NEVER FRET, because Mr. Maguire was a fiddle player. He taught lessons over in Winter Beach at the JAM School of Music and played at Winter Beach restaurants some nights. There were two lawn chairs parked outside under an awning. One of the lawn chairs had a deep impression in the middle; that one was Mr. Maguire's.

I bounded up the two steps and knocked, bobbing from foot to foot while I waited.

The door flung open. "Scout!"

I loved Declan's nickname for me. It came from the book *To Kill a Mockingbird*, which he loved so much he insisted I read it. Scout was the narrator of the story; she was a scrappy girl, who probably looked a lot like me and needed to understand the injustice her daddy was fighting. It was a good book, and a compliment to be called Scout. "What's kickin', chicken?" I asked, even though Declan looked more like a rooster than a chicken, with his red hair.

"Get in here, Scout. It's too hot outside. Want a lime-ade spritzer to cool off?"

21

I did.

Our trailers were similar, except the Maguire trailer was loaded with stuff. Musical instruments and albums that belonged to Mr. Maguire and tons of cooking equipment—colorful bowls that were chipped here and there, an old blender, a dented metal colander, large spoons for stirring and scooping—that belonged to Declan.

I sat on the bench at the kitchen table and sneaked a peek at Declan's computer. He'd been watching a cooking video on YouTube.

Declan stuck his head into the fridge and came out with a lime from Weezie's Market and Flower Emporium; I knew that because there was no other food store in town. Winter Beach had a farmers' market on Saturdays, but only in wintertime. Occasionally Mr. Maguire took me and Declan there and treated us to lunch from one of the vendors. We always ate on a picnic table near the stage with live music. Mr. Maguire never forgot to put a handful of dollar bills in the musicians' tip jar before we left.

I checked in my bag to make sure everything was there while Dec rummaged around in a cabinet near the sink and pulled out a small juicer, a cutting board, a bottle of agave—his favorite sweetener—and a pitcher.

He reached into a drawer and extracted a big knife and grabbed a bottle of seltzer.

I tapped my toes and nibbled on a fingernail. "I only have, like, ten minutes, Dec."

He stopped slicing the lime and glanced over at me. Because of his recent start-of-school haircut, Declan's ears seemed to protrude more than usual, which he hated but I thought was adorable. He looked like a Vulcan from that old TV show *Star Trek*. "Where you heading in such a big hurry?"

I held up my bag. "Ballet school with Miss Delilah. Remember?"

Declan's mouth stretched into a smile that seemed to make the freckles on his cheeks stand out. "This is really happening, Scout. You're going to do it."

I nodded. "First item on the list."

Dec came over and gave me a hard fist bump. "That's how it's done."

I smelled tangy lime, and little bubbles of possibility floated through me—like even a twelve-year-old girl from Sassafras, Florida, could really make it to Paris, France.

Declan finished making the limeade and poured it into cups.

We clinked our cups. "To Paris," he said.

"To Paris!" I swigged the sweet, tart fizzy drink. *And to best friends.*

I left Declan's trailer filled with happiness. It was always like that with Dec. I was sad over the reason he and his dad had to move to our trailer park when Dec was in third grade, but glad they were here now. Really glad, especially after my supposed friend Jenna Finch dumped me. Declan would never think I wasn't good enough for him, even after what happened to Dad. He was a true friend.

Clutching my bag of clothes, I speed-walked all the way to Miss Delilah's School of Dance and Fine Pottery, ready to show those ballet girls I could twirl and plié and leap as good as they could. Just because they lived in the nicer part of town with the fancy houses didn't make them better than me. I knew Jenna would be in the class. She's taken ballet every year since she was little. A tiny part of me hoped that when Jenna saw me there, she'd remember some of the reasons we became friends in the first place. Because we'd be outside of school, maybe she'd start talking to me again. Laughing with me. Wanting my friendship back.

Since the older kids' class was at five o'clock, I got to see the little girls in leotards from the earlier class stream out the door and into the parking lot to meet their moms.

I gave silent thanks to Georgia for making sure I wasn't stuck in a class with them. Imagine me towering over all those little kids. That would have been *très* embarrassing.

A metallic-blue BMW swung into a parking spot, narrowly missing one of the bitty ballerinas. I recognized that car.

Jenna Finch stepped out of the passenger side and slammed the door.

I inhaled so sharply that I choked on my own spit.

Jenna slung her pink duffel over her shoulder and headed toward the dance school without a glance in my direction.

Bonjour, Jenna! "Hi, Jenna." I rushed up to her, painfully aware that her shiny brown hair was in a tight bun with no stray pieces, and mine was a sweaty mess under my beret. I had tried to make the bobby pins work, but they kept poking my scalp, and my hair wouldn't stay put. It was hopeless. I wished Mom or Georgia were home to help, but they were both working and now my hair didn't look like it was supposed to.

Jenna's mom probably helped her achieve the ideal ballerina bun.

Parfait! Perfect!

Jenna pivoted toward me. Her bun, I noticed, didn't move a millimeter.

25

My heart sped up. Jenna was looking right at me, like I actually existed.

"Hey, Cleveland," she said, easy as key lime pie, as though she hadn't ignored me all of sixth grade, all summer, and today at school. "What are you doing here?" Jenna stood near the door and stretched her right leg up toward her head. It made a tiny clicking sound. "You don't take ballet," she said into her kneecap. "Right?"

I lifted my paper bag to show Jenna I had all the things I needed to take ballet, but then I lowered it and slid the bag behind my back. *Why didn't I think of buying a pink duffel like she has?* "I'm signed up for class now." My heart hammered. *What can I say to make her like me again?* I pretended to feel bright and cheerful. "Advanced ballet." *Just like you.*

Jenna stretched her other leg in the air for a few moments. *How does she do that? Will I have to do that?* I felt woozy—my legs might break off if I attempted those moves. Then who would walk Miss Genevieve and Scarlett Bananas? *Maybe advanced ballet wasn't the best idea.*

"I didn't know you could do that," Jenna said.

I thought of Georgia fighting for me to be able to join this class and how I had to show Miss Delilah that I knew the ballet positions. "Well, you can," I offered helpfully.

Jenna looked me up and down. "Okay then." She flung open the door and walked into the cool air, leaving me standing out front, with my messy hair and my ballet clothes in a paper bag; my bubble of happiness popped.

I took a long, slow breath for bravery like Georgia taught me and reminded myself how important the Paris Project was. I had started planning it because of how Jenna treated me after she moved; then it felt more important than ever with what happened with Dad. There was only one way to get to Paris, and that was by completing each item on the list. Then I would be ready (and hopefully have saved enough money). So I opened the door and marched across the chilly lobby, past Miss Delilah's office, past the studio, and into the changing room.

A bunch of girls were already in there, adjusting their leotards and stuffing clothing and pink duffel bags into lockers.

"Hey, Jenna," Nicole Kyle said. "I so don't feel like dancing today."

"Me neither." Jenna cracked her neck. "Let's go home."

"Okay."

Both girls laughed as they put on their ballet slippers.

I placed my bag on a bench near a row of lockers and

pulled on my new tights, careful not to poke a finger-nail through them and cause a run. Luckily, I chewed my fingernails, so there wasn't too much nail left to make that happen.

When everyone was dressed, they walked to the stu-dio. Jenna led the pack. I followed at the rear, shiver-ing, but not from the air-conditioning. This was really happening. I was going to complete the first item on my list!

Wearing my new leotard, tights, and ballet slippers, I felt like a real ballerina. And my beret made me feel like a French ballerina, so everything was perfect as I approached the studio at Miss Delilah's School of Dance and Fine Pottery.

From the doorway, I noticed there were no boys in the group. *Zut! Who will toss me into the air?* None of the girls looked hearty enough to do it without dropping me on my head.

As soon as I entered the space with the wood floors, mirrored wall, and long barre, Miss Delilah called out, "Come here, please, Cleveland."

Maybe she wanted to welcome me to the "family" or tell me some rules since I was new.

Miss Delilah put her hand on my shoulder and said in a soft voice, "Cleveland?"

"Yeah?" I smiled big, even though I had an embarrassing space between my two top front teeth. I wanted her to know how happy I was to be there.

The other girls were at the barre stretching, but I saw them sneaking glimpses at me and felt my cheeks heat up. I wanted to be stretching at the barre with them, like a real ballerina who might someday be performing onstage at a Parisian theater, with patrons tossing roses at her feet and shouting, *"Magnifique!"*

"I'm going to be your ballet teacher for this class." Miss Delilah did not let go of my shoulder. My impulse was to shrug her hand off, but I could feel the girls staring and didn't want to mess things up on my first day, especially in front of Jenna.

"That means"—her grip tightened a smidge—"what I say in this class goes."

I nodded. And maybe grimaced a little too. I didn't understand why Miss Delilah was saying that. Of course I was going to listen to whatever she said. I wanted to be the best one in the whole class.

"And I say you absolutely, positively may not wear that hat in my class."

It's called a beret. "But—"

"I told you already that you either had to wear your hair in a bun or pin it up as best you can. You've chosen to do neither." She finally let go of my poor shoulder and bent so she was a little above me, but looking directly in my eyes. "What if that thing were to fall off and cause a problem?"

"Oh, don't worry about that." I finally understood what this was about. "It *never* falls off." I patted the top of my beret. "It's on there like superglue. Promise. I tried the pins, but they wouldn't work on my hair. It's too fine."

Miss Delilah forced air from her flared nostrils, but it wasn't in the relaxed way Georgia had taught me when I needed to calm down. Some of those disgusting air molecules from Miss Delilah's nose rained down on my forehead. I wanted to run into the bathroom and scrub my forehead clean, but I stayed still, like I was practicing to be a statue at the Louvre. "Well, we can't take that chance. Can we?"

I took a tiny step backward, away from her stream of gross nose air.

Yes, we can! "I, um . . ." My voice dropped to a whisper. I didn't want to talk about this, but I understood she wasn't going to let it go too easily, and I was eager to join the other girls and start dancing. "Miss Delilah?" A couple of hot tears pricked the corners of my eyes. "I never take this beret off." I didn't tell Miss Delilah I took it off to shower and sleep, because that particular information was none of her business, plus it wouldn't help my case. "Because . . ." I might have let one or two of those tears spill over on purpose. "Because . . . it's from my dad." I said that last part a little too loudly. Even though I was upset with my dad for what he did, I missed him so much . . . and somehow wearing the beret made me feel like he was there with me, instead of where he really was.

The other girls were openly staring and whispering behind their hands now. I even heard a couple of gasps. I wished Georgia were here. She wouldn't let Miss Delilah talk to me like this. She'd make sure I could wear my beret, which wasn't hurting a single person.

Miss Delilah stood there, looking at me over the frame of her glasses.

My beret suddenly felt like it weighed as much as the whole stupid town of Sassafras, but I stood there, under the weight of it all, watched by every girl in class and Miss Delilah, with what could only be described as expressions of pity.

Pity!

The last thing I needed was someone feeling sorry for me. I was Cleveland Rosebud Potts—destined for Paris— and I certainly didn't need anyone's dumb pity face!

Miss Delilah touched her index finger to a mole on her cheek. "Let it not be said I don't have charity in my heart. I'm going to allow you to wear the hat this time. Before the next class, though, I will personally help you pin your hair up. And, Cleveland, even the good Lord above won't be able to help you if that thing falls off your stubborn little head during my class."

I shook my stubborn little head. "Won't fall off." My voice came out sounding small and weak, instead of strong and firm, like I'd intended.

Miss Delilah pushed her glasses up on her nose and said in a fake-sympathetic voice, "We're all real sorry for the unfortunate circumstance of your daddy. Aren't we, girls?"

I hated that people in Sassafras knew everything about everyone else, especially the things you didn't want them to know. Most especially when those things were written about in the local newspaper because certain awful things that recently happened to our family were a matter of public record. Everyone in town knew that my dad stole money from his boss, Mr. Ronnie Baker, at the auto supply store. That fact was proven beyond a shadow of a doubt in court. What the busybodies in town didn't know was that my dad took money from me, too, after he stole the money from his boss. I wasn't about to tell any of them. They also knew exactly where my dad was now. And that was the most embarrassing part.

The girls nodded like bobblehead ballet dolls, except for Jenna Finch, who busted out laughing. *Laughing!*

Nicole shoved her shoulder, but it was too late.

It set off a chain reaction.

Almost all the girls were giggling behind their hands.

Giggling.

Laughing.

Laughing!

I didn't deserve to be snickered at by a bunch of dopey ballet girls with perfect buns on their heads because of Dad's actions. This was what I'd been worried about. Why couldn't I go to a dance class without having to be reminded? Was I more upset with them for laughing at me or with Dad for what he'd done that made everything harder? Angry feelings whirled inside me, like they were spinning in some kind of internal emotion blender, and I couldn't figure out what feelings were caused by which people.

Part of me wanted to flee from the room, but my stiff new size-ten ballet slippers felt cemented to the floor. No way would I give these girls the satisfaction of that happening. I was just as good as every one of those bunheads.

It wasn't my fault my dad resided at Wayside Correctional Institution in Babcock Lakes, Florida, a town so tiny the population was 1,236.

"Enough!" Miss Delilah clapped her hands three times. "Let's get to work, ladies!"

I forced myself to walk to the barre with the rest of the class, who'd finally stopped laughing, and then I stared darts at the back of Jenna Finch's perfect bunhead. Why couldn't that girl be nice to me? Didn't all our years of being friends mean anything? We used to have so much fun together—playing marathon Monopoly games with me and my dad and horsing around in the pool as Dad performed crazy cannonballs into the water, or the times he took us out for ice cream at Snazzy's Snack Shack. Didn't Jenna remember all those good times we had? Didn't they matter to her?

Even though my cheeks felt like they were on fire . . . even though I was the only person in that whole room with an incarcerated parent . . . even though I could barely hold my head up from all the shame that filled it . . . I would stay there and be a true, poised French ballerina. Then I would leave all of them in Sassafras dust.

My project was going to work. It had to. It was the only way to get away from these awful feelings.

Small Things Can Cause Big Pain

"LINE UP. BACKS STRAIGHT. PRETEND there's a string being pulled from the tops of your heads. That's it. Perfect!"

Parfait, I thought. Everything will be *parfait* . . . someday.

As Miss Delilah called out positions, I worked hard to keep up with the other girls, making my body move like the ballerinas I'd studied in the videos. It took extra effort because I was also holding back tears, but that was okay. I could do anything they did, only better and with more panache!

I glanced at myself in the mirror while holding on to the barre. There I was—Cleveland Rosebud

Potts—wearing a brand-new leotard, tights, and ballet slippers. The beret made me look *très chic*, if you want my honest opinion. I was staring back at a real ballerina. So excited about how I looked, I almost winked at myself but didn't want to give the girls another reason to laugh at me. Besides, I wasn't very good at winking. Instead I held myself as tall as I could and let my inner ballerina sparkle.

"Okay, ladies," Miss Delilah said. "Now that you're warmed up, let's step away from the barre and work on our pirouettes."

I walked across the floor to practice spinning on one foot.

I couldn't help peering at myself again to make sure I still looked like a real ballerina. I did! As I spun, I imagined myself onstage at a Parisian theater, twirling into the arms of a ballet dancer who would toss me in the air, as though I weighed less than a bag of snack-size Cheetos Puffs.

I felt freer with each revolution. All my problems fell away as I spun and spun. A few spins, pause, spin.

Ballet was fun.

Spinning.

Spinning.

Spinnnnnnnnnnnnnnnnnnning. Wheeeee!

"Cleveland Potts!"

"Huh?"

I stopped spinning and looked around, but the world continued to whirl. Everyone was back at the barre while I'd been in the center of the room, spinning. Alone. With everyone glaring at me. How had I missed the instructions to stop spinning?

Humiliant!

I had to get back to the barre, but the floor swayed beneath me, making walking nearly impossible. When I managed to get close, I leaned over and felt my beret slip. I reached up to grab it, but I must have accidentally touched Jenna Finch's arm, because she screeched, "Get off me!"

"Sorry." I hadn't meant to touch her, but I wanted to keep my beret from falling. Too late.

It was on the floor; I made a grab for it before Miss Delilah noticed. Everything spun inside my head, which made everything spin inside my stomach, too. I struggled to keep from hurling a partially digested peanut butter and jelly sandwich and mini carrots from lunch onto my brand-new size-ginormous ballet slippers.

"Oh, I'll get your stupid hat," Jenna said.

But I was headed for the floor an instant before she bent down.

Jenna tumbled over me, her long, flexible legs flipping up behind her.

One of her feet banged into the barre hard enough that I heard it connect. *Crack!*

We ended up in a very ungraceful heap.

I sat up and blinked a few times, glad my stomach had mostly settled.

Jenna sat across from me, cradling her foot in her hand, rocking back and forth and wailing.

"Oh, good Lord!" Miss Delilah shouted as she approached the gaggle of girls surrounding Jenna. She peeled off Jenna's ballet slipper, which made Jenna shriek.

"Jenna, you'd better get those tights off so I can get a good look at your foot."

"Nooooo! My toe! Cleveland broke my toe!"

A few girls turned to glare at me.

Tiny bumps sprang up across my arms. This was the second time I'd wanted to run away in a matter of minutes.

"Oh, for Pete's sake, Jenna. Your toe's not broken," Miss Delilah scolded. "Don't be so melodramatic. Now, take your tights off so I can look at it. Probably just needs ice on it, is all."

Jenna, with two girls holding her up, hobbled toward

the changing room. The other girls followed them. Silence settled like broken glass between Miss Delilah and me while we waited. Those were the longest minutes of my life. Not the worst minutes, but the longest. I hoped Jenna was okay. Even though she didn't want to be my friend anymore, I didn't want her toe to be broken. I knew how much ballet meant to her. She loved wearing the costumes and performing at the recitals and had often practiced her routines when we used to hang out.

Jenna eventually hobbled back, wearing her leotard with no tights. The other girls had worried looks on their pinched-up faces.

"Oh," Miss Delilah said. "Ohhhh."

I bit the skin at the edge of my thumbnail.

Jenna's pinkie toe had swelled and purpled up like a little eggplant, the kind they sometimes sold in wooden crates at Weezie's Market and Flower Emporium. Declan called the vegetable crates "Weezie's fancy-pants foods section," and he'd buy up whatever was in them and make some kind of delicious stew. Even if you hated eggplant or didn't know exactly what it was, you'd love the stew Declan made from it, because that boy could cook as good as any famous chef.

"We should call your mom," Miss Delilah said in a hushed tone. "I think your toe's broken."

Jenna wailed with renewed zeal.

I attacked the skin next to my thumbnail with equal zeal.

Miss Delilah and the girls encircled her, and then Miss Delilah looked back at me. "Cleveland, get dressed and gather your things. I'm calling your mom too." She shook her head, causing her beaded eyeglass chain to rattle. "Good Lord, child, you certainly are something!"

I squeezed the beret in my right fist. *May all your dreams come true, baby girl,* Dad had said to me when he gave me the beret for my eleventh birthday. But now the beret was causing me a big problem. *Gros problème!* After squeezing the life out of it, I jammed it back on. Even though it shouldn't have, the beret somehow made me feel better, less alone.

I watched the chosen ballerinas support Jenna and follow Miss Delilah toward her office; the other girls huddled close behind them, like baby ducklings following their mama.

This was not good.

This. Was. Not. Good.

Ce n'était pas bon.

Sins of the Father

SAT ON ONE OF THE three hard plastic chairs in the lobby, clutching the bag with my ballet clothes in it and shivering. This time it was from the AC. I never understood why the inside of every single building and store in Sassafras felt like you'd stepped into a refrigerator. Georgia had to wear long sleeves at work, even when it was over ninety degrees outside.

I'd read that most people in Paris didn't have air-conditioning because they didn't need it. The temperatures in Paris were ideal most of the year. Too bad I was stuck in Sassafras.

I slumped in my seat.

Through the front window, I looked across the

highway at the closed-down gas station—GAS, GRUB, 'N GO. It had been shut down as long as I could remember, and nothing ever showed up to replace it, like an animal shelter or a movie theater. I thought about the other stores along the strip where Miss Delilah's school was: a Chinese restaurant that never seemed to be open, Ronnie's Auto Supplies & Service (where Mom used to buy things to fix up our car, Miss Lola Lemon, but now, because of what happened, she'll have to order parts online or get them from a supply shop all the way in Winter Beach—*thanks a lot, Dad*), an insurance office or a real estate office—I couldn't remember which—and Patty's Pampered Pets (which was fun because I could watch the dogs getting a bath through the window). There were also three empty stores that I wished would open up as something interesting, like a bookstore or a tea shop or a French bakery. As if places like that would ever come to Sassafras!

A quick movement in the parking lot caught my attention. Jenna's mom's BMW nearly plowed down an unsuspecting squirrel; he leaped out of the way to avoid being flattened as the car swerved into a parking spot. She might have run over the tip of his bushy tail.

Poor squirrel.

Wearing a sleeveless top and a bouncy white tennis

skirt with a purple stripe, Jenna's mom marched in. "What's this all about?" she said to no one.

I pretended to be invisible, and it worked. Jenna's mom's eyes slid right over me and focused on Miss Delilah's office door, which she opened without knocking.

"Jenna!" I heard through the now-closed door. "Your toe! It's humongous!"

"Oh, Lord." Miss Delilah's voice.

After some crying and loud voices, which I couldn't clearly make out, Ms. Finch and Jenna, who was leaning on her and hopping, came out of the office. That was when Ms. Finch noticed me. "Is this who did it?" She scrunched up her face as though I were a glop of just-discovered dog poo under her expensive tennis shoe.

Jenna sniffled and nodded.

"Figures."

What was that supposed to mean? I pushed back into my chair as hard as I could and stared lasers at the visor perched on her suntanned forehead.

"Cleveland Potts!" Ms. Finch was so close to my face that I saw beads of sweat on her upper lip, which I couldn't understand how, considering how cold it was in there. "Look here," she said. "I'm truly sorry about what's going on with your daddy, but that's not a reason

43

to go around hurting other people. You don't need to act bad because he did."

My stomach twisted into a thousand knots. *I would never do what my dad did.* I took a shaky breath, then exploded: "It was an accident, lady!"

"Mm-hmm."

I wanted to shove past her and run all the way to Declan's trailer, where we'd go back to sipping lime-ade spritzers, and I'd listen to him call me Scout, like I meant something.

Miss Delilah forced her body between Jenna's mom and me. "Cleveland, please go into my office. Your mom's on her way." She faced Ms. Finch. "We'll continue our discussion soon."

"Oh, yes we will." Then Ms. Finch swiveled and gave Jenna a yank on the elbow that made her wince. "That girl's always been jealous of you."

Me? Jealous of Jenna? Ha! Ms. Finch didn't know what she was talking about, but I decided not to tell her just then. I was still boiling from what she'd said about my dad.

Jenna limped out of the dance school with her mom, and I could hardly believe what I saw: the bun at the back of Jenna's head was perfectly undisturbed.

It was a shame her pinkie toe looked like a miniature hot dog about to explode from its casing.

After the awful things Jenna's mom said, I felt like a car that had run out of gas. I wasn't bad. Even though my dad did some bad things, he did a lot of good things too. He fixed people's cars sometimes without charging them, if he knew they couldn't afford it. He once brought a whole bag of groceries over to Mr. Jenks's trailer when he'd hurt his back and couldn't work for a while. And if me or Mom or Georgia was having a bad day, Dad always told jokes to make us laugh away our foul moods. He even let our dog up on the bed at night because he couldn't resist Miss Genevieve's sad eyes. Did the couple of bad things Dad did erase all the good things before that? Was he really bad? The state of Florida sure seemed to think he was. But to me, I wasn't so sure.

I could barely muster the energy to follow Miss Delilah into her office.

I sat in one of the chairs across from Miss Delilah's desk. The same place I sat when Georgia signed me up only three weeks ago, back when everything sparkled with possibility.

Miss Delilah busied herself with a bunch of papers on her desk.

I heard the clock on the wall above my head tick-tick-ticking as I waited for Mom to show up. With each tick, I imagined how upset she would be with me because I

45

caused her to leave work. She'd also be mad about what Ms. Finch said about Dad, but I wouldn't tell her that. Mom had enough to deal with.

Miss Delilah glanced up at the clock and sighed.

I tapped my toes on the floor in time with the ticking clock.

Tap. Tap. Tap. Tap.

Finally Mom peeked around the open door, as if not sure she was in the right place.

Seeing Mom triggered a rush of emotions—worry that she'd be mad at me and relief because I finally had someone who'd be on my side. A few tears leaked out, but I brushed them away with the back of my hand.

Mom wore her MARVELOUS MAIDS AT YOUR SERVICE T-shirt tucked into old jeans, and her hair was pulled into a messy ponytail of wild black curls. Honestly, she looked like she'd been scrubbing somebody's toilet.

I slunk low in my seat.

"Please." Miss Delilah pointed toward the chair next to mine. "Join us."

Mom wiped her palms on her thighs and sat.

Miss Delilah pressed her palms onto the papers on her desk. "I'm sorry to tell you this, but Cleveland ended up hurting another student during our class today."

"But I didn't do it on—"

"Cleveland!" Mom snapped. "Let Miss Delilah finish talking."

I sank lower.

"As I was saying . . ." Miss Delilah pushed her glasses up on her nose. "I don't think Cleveland did this on purpose, no matter what the mother of the other girl says. But Cleveland's actions caused another student to have quite a tumble. And now it seems that student has a broken toe."

"It was only a pinkie toe," I mumbled.

"Cleveland Potts," Mom warned.

"Sorry." I wished I could pull my beret down over my whole face and leave it that way.

"The bottom line is"—Miss Delilah cleared her throat—"I don't think Cleveland is ready for ballet."

"Wait! What?" I bolted upright. "But . . ."

Miss Delilah reached into her drawer, pulled out five twenty-dollar bills, and handed them to my mom. "I'm returning the money Georgia gave me for the lessons."

Mom accepted the money, her lips pressed tight.

"I can't refund the registration fee."

Mom didn't say anything.

"On account of it's nonrefundable."

Mom continued looking at Miss Delilah until she reached into her drawer and handed her another twenty. *That* made me glad, at least, because it was

47

Georgia's money, after all. But I couldn't be kicked out of ballet. I. Could. Not.

"I'll be better. I'll try harder. I'll—"

Mom silenced me with a glare.

It felt like a boulder was crushing my heart. I had to accomplish the items on my Paris Project list. I *had* to!

Mom stood. "Thank you. Cleveland and I are very sorry for what happened to that girl's toe. Aren't we, Cleveland?"

I nodded hard, but not hard enough to knock my beret off, because I didn't want to deal with that disaster again. And not hard enough to shake out the tears that had welled up and were trying to bust loose.

Mom turned toward me. "Let's go, Cleveland. We'll talk in the car."

I gulped.

"Thank you, Miss Delilah," I whispered, even though I wasn't sure what I was thanking her for. "May-maybe I'll come back to take classes another time."

She gave her head a shake so big it dislodged the glasses from her nose.

"Or not."

I followed Mom out of Miss Delilah's School of Dance and Fine Pottery, where I never did see any pottery, fine or otherwise.

Pinkie Toes Are Highly Overrated

THE PASSENGER DOOR ON MOM'S car didn't open because the handle had broken off a while ago, and Mom said it was a nonessential, so I had to crawl through the driver's side. The hand brake poked me as I climbed over, and I felt like I deserved it. I shoved the bag of ballet clothes onto the floor in the backseat, angry at all the money I'd paid for them . . . for absolutely nothing. There wasn't another dance school in Sassafras, so unless someone wanted to drive me all the way to Winter Beach for classes, that bag of clothes would go unused and probably reside under my bed forever. No one would be able to drive me to Winter Beach for classes.

I considered asking Mom if she'd go back in and demand a refund on my clothes. Then I looked at her faded jeans, her dirty T-shirt, and the thin line of her lips pressed together and knew better than to let those words out of my mouth. I'd have to eat the cost of everything, even those pokey bobby pins that never worked on my hair.

Mom was eerily quiet as she backed Miss Lola Lemon out of the parking lot and drove away from Miss Delilah's dance school.

"Are we going home?" I hoped so because I was ready to cuddle up near Miss Genevieve and be left alone for a while to figure this whole mess out and think more about my list. Or maybe I would go over to Declan's again and see what he was cooking. Maybe he'd make me another limeade spritzer. I sure could use one.

"Nope," Mom said.

We drove along a road that was flanked by overgrown weeds and passed a huge sign that read WORM FARM— COME TRY OUR NEW WORM TEA! *(Um, no thank you! I bet they don't sell worm tea in France!)* "Mom, really, where are we going?"

For a hopeful second, I wished Mom would take me to Pamela's Pancake House, because of how badly everyone treated me at the dance school. Pamela's was one of our favorite celebrating places. Our other favorite place was in Winter Beach—Margaret Mitchell's Restaurant—but we only went there once. Of course Mom had no idea how mean everyone had been to me today, and we probably couldn't afford to eat at Pamela's, especially because Mom would want to buy an extra dinner to bring home to Georgia.

And we definitely weren't going to Margaret Mitchell's, because that place was *très* expensive! Five times more expensive than Pamela's. But it was so good.

Dad had taken all of us there once—even Declan—because Dad won *a lot* of money at the dog park that night.

"Order anything you want," Dad had said when we were seated in wooden chairs with silk-covered cushions. It was so fancy we laid white cloth napkins on our laps. I sat extra tall in my chair; something about the place made me feel important. Even though Jenna wasn't talking to me then, I still felt great sitting there at Margaret Mitchell's with my family and Declan. That was because I had no idea what was about to happen to us.

"Anything?" I had whispered. "Even drinks?" We were only allowed to ask for water when we went out to eat, which we almost never did; water didn't cost extra.

"Especially drinks!" Dad seemed as jolly and generous as Santa Claus.

I could tell he was enjoying doing this for all of us. I wondered if we'd start eating at places like this more often. Maybe we'd even end up getting a house on the hill in town like Jenna and her family did.

Dad's eyes were wide with excitement. Mom smiled so hard, the skin beside her eyes wrinkled. Georgia kept nudging me, like she couldn't believe it was happening. And Declan looked blissful. I wished we could have brought Miss Genevieve so the whole family could be there, but this wasn't the kind of place you brought a dog.

The owners, Craig and William, introduced themselves and said they hoped we'd have a wonderful time at their establishment. They wore old-fashioned suits with top hats and something called spats over their shoes. Declan asked what they were. William explained that spats were a covering worn to protect shoes and socks from rain and mud splatter until about the 1920s. Declan nodded like he was in a trance. I had a feeling he wished he could wear spats over his sneakers right then.

The restaurant was decorated like it came out of the 1920s. Old-fashioned jazz music played through speakers hidden among the decorations, like an antique telephone with a dial and a piece you held up to your ear, a record player that had a big megaphone attached to it, and a bunch of lamps with beautiful stained-glass covers.

I elbowed Declan. "Isn't this the coolest place?"

He was staring at William and Craig, who were behind a marble counter, talking and laughing. "Huh?"

I shook my head at him. "What're you going to order, Dec?"

He pulled his eyes away from the pair. "Um, let me check." He opened his menu, but then his gaze wandered back to the men again.

I figured Declan wanted to be like them and own a cool restaurant someday.

"Well, I'm getting the truffle mac and cheese," I said, even though Declan wasn't paying attention.

"Uh-huh. Sounds good." He wasn't even looking at the menu anymore.

Georgia held up her menu and whispered to me behind it. "I wish Dad would win big like this all the time."

"Me too," I said.

Now I understood what gambling all the time could make an otherwise good person do.

Mom tapped on Lola Lemon's steering wheel, which brought me back, out of my thoughts. "I'm pretty mad right now, Cleveland Potts," she said.

Not going to Pamela's Pancake House. Definitely not going to Margaret Mitchell's.

"Did you know I had to call Charlene Walters to come finish cleaning the house I was working in?"

"Sorry," I muttered, although you'd think Mom would be at least a little happy I got her out of cleaning someone else's dirty house.

"Know what that means, kiddo?"

You don't have to clean someone else's stinkin' house? I shook my head.

Mom glanced at me, then focused on the road ahead. "It means I have to pay Charlene the full fee for doing me the favor on such short notice, even though I'd already been cleaning for well over an hour and had done both bathrooms. When Miss Delilah called and told me I'd better get to the school right away, I thought you had a terrible accident, Cleveland. Then she explained you'd hurt that Jenna Finch girl, and I was really puzzled because, honey, that's not like you at all. And now we have to drive back to the house I was working at so I can pay Charlene all the money my client had already paid me. When Miss Delilah called, I rushed right out and didn't even wait for Charlene to show up."

I bit the skin around my thumbnail. "I'm sorry you had to leave work because of me."

54

"I appreciate it, but your sorry doesn't put that money back in my pocket."

I leaned my head against the partially open sun-warmed window and squinted, pretending we were passing a Parisian cheese shop, an outdoor café, and a fancy hat store instead of a sporting goods shop, a McDonald's, and a Walmart Superstore. *Très chic!*

"Cleve?"

"Yeah?" I didn't have the strength to lift my head.

"I need to know, honey. Did you hurt that Finch girl on purpose?"

"No!" I leaned forward. How could she even think that? "I'm not saying she didn't deserve it." I couldn't tell Mom that Jenna had laughed at what happened to Dad. She would be really upset. "I got really dizzy from spinning, and then I tipped over. That's all."

"That's all? Why were you spinning, Cleveland?"

"We were supposed to. Sort of."

"Sort of?" Mom made an extra-hard turn.

"We were supposed to stop doing pirouettes, I guess, but I didn't hear that part and I got dizzy. Then"—I breathed in tiny gasps, the exact opposite of how I was supposed to calm myself down—"my beret fell off and . . ." I thought about how Miss Delilah tried to make me take it off before class, and a few hot tears dribbled

55

down my cheeks. I swiped at them with the backs of my hands. "It was a weird accident, Mom. I swear on everything French. Somehow, Jenna tripped over me; she flipped up really fast and smashed her pinkie toe on the barre. I heard it crack."

"The barre?"

"No. Her toe."

"Oh my. That must've hurt like a son of a grass-hopper."

"Yeah. Her little toe blew up like a purple eggplant, but I didn't mean for that to happen. I'd smash my own pinkie toe if I could undo everything." I released a whoosh of air and leaned back.

Mom patted my knee. "Cleveland Rosebud Potts?"

I liked when Mom used my middle name. "Yeah?"

"Pinkie toes are highly overrated."

"Pinkie toes are . . ." I burst out laughing.

Mom laughed too. Her laughter was the best sound I'd heard all day.

I leaned my head on her shoulder for a second. It smelled faintly of bleach.

"Seriously, Cleve," Mom said. "There's nothing that can be done for a broken toe. That girl'll just have to ice and elevate it. She'll be okay. I bet she'll be dancing again in no time. Someone told me it takes about seven weeks for a broken toe to heal. That's not too terrible. Right?"

I shrugged. Jenna might get to dance again in seven weeks, but I wouldn't. Because apparently, I was no longer welcome at Miss Delilah's School of Dance and Fine Pottery. "Want to know something strange?"

"Hmm?" She kept her eyes on the road.

"Jenna had a perfect bun through all of it, Mom."

She tapped the steering wheel with her index finger. "They always do, baby girl, because they spray their hair within an inch of its life. It never moves. Never. The hair of those dance girls would probably survive a category four hurricane without a single strand popping out of place."

I laughed again, even though hurricanes weren't funny business, and I never wanted to live through another one. Hurricanes were plain scary, when they weren't being the most boring things ever because school was closed and there was usually no electricity and nothing to do except melt in the sticky heat. I reminded myself to look into getting some kind of hair spray, because it might help my hair do something more interesting than droop and play dead.

Relaxing into my seat, I waited for Mom to state my punishment. There would be some kind of punishment for hurting someone, causing a ruckus, and making Mom miss work.

But Mom surprised me by not saying anything. She kept driving, like it was any other day.

Then she pulled into the driveway of a nice house that had a front porch with a swing on it. I bet there were two or three big dogs living there. And maybe a parakeet or a pig or some other kind of pet that rich people liked to have.

"I'm just going to run the money up to Charlene and talk to her for a few minutes," Mom said.

"Okay."

"And Cleveland?"

"Yeah?"

"Georgia has to work, but I scheduled an appointment for you and me to see Dad this Sunday at the video visitation center."

"But—"

"Don't even . . ." Then Mom slammed the car door and jogged up the steps to that fancy house, with three dogs and maybe a parakeet and a pig inside.

It was so hot in the car that I opened Mom's door and prayed for a breeze. Living in Sassafras, Florida, was fourteen flavors of miserable. And after this news I felt like I was suffocating. I couldn't believe Mom made an appointment for me to visit Dad without even asking me. What if I didn't want to?

Visit . . . my dad.

In jail.

And there it was.

The punishment.

I'd already visited four times since Dad went in on June 30, and that had been four times too many. Why couldn't Mom understand? I shouldn't have to go there and be reminded . . . of everything I'd lost. My money for Paris. My dog-walking customers. My friends. Everything . . . including my dad. *Mostly Dad.* It hurt to see him there. It felt easier not to see him at all.

I made myself think happy thoughts. Practicing French while walking Miss Genevieve, him wagging his stump of a tail with joy. Hanging out with Declan while he created a scrumptious meal from his special cook-book. Dancing with Georgia in our trailer, even though she didn't have time for that nowadays. Imagining attending the American School of Paris . . . someday.

Or maybe not.

I couldn't even accomplish the first item on my Paris Project list. I wiped sweat off my forehead with my palm. If I couldn't survive the first item on my list, how would I ever get through the more difficult items?

Je suis irritée. So, so irritated!

While Mom did whatever in the rich people's house

with all the pets they might or might not have, I reached over into the glove compartment and pulled out a copy of my Paris Project list and a purple pen. I kept one copy in the car, another copy in my backpack, and a third in my bedroom so I'd always have it nearby to remind me of my big goal and the things I'd have to accomplish to reach it. I had planned to stick another copy on the fridge with our Rock & Roll Hall of Fame magnet, but now I was too embarrassed to put it where everyone could see that I'd failed right from the start.

I smoothed out the paper and read the first item, then bit my bottom lip. I imagined a big red stamp over it with a single word: *Failure!* Since I didn't have a big red stamp, I slashed a line through it, put the paper and pen away, and slumped in Mom's seat. I reminded myself to do the same thing to the other two copies when I got home.

Failure in triplicate.

Mom came out of the house and down the steps. I was glad because even with the car door wide open, the heat was making me wilt. I scooted back over to my seat and wiped sweat off my upper lip.

Trying to bloom when you were planted in a place like Sassafras, Florida, was not the easiest thing in the world, even if your name was Cleveland *Rosebud* Potts.

The Paris Project
By Cleveland Rosebud Potts

~~1. Take ballet lessons at Miss Delilah's School of Dance and Fine Pottery (to acquire some culture).~~

2. Learn to cook at least one French dish and eat at a French restaurant (to be prepared for the real thing).

3. Take in paintings by the French impressionists, like Claude Monet's *Water-Lily Pond*, at an art museum so I can experience what good French art is (more culture!).

4. Continue learning to speak French (will come in handy when moving to France and needing to find important places, like *la salle de bains*, so I can go *oui oui*—ha-ha!—French bathroom humor).

5. Apply to the American School of Paris (must earn full scholarship to attend for eighth grade. You can do this, Cleveland!).

6. Move to France! *(Fini!)*

Good riddance, Sassafras, Florida!

The Summer of Shame

I T WAS ALMOST DARK BY the time we got home. Frogs croaked in the nearby canal. I smelled someone's spicy dinner cooking, and my stomach rumbled. The last thing I'd eaten was a peanut butter and jelly sandwich at lunch a looooong time ago.

Mom and I crunched along the gravel to our trailer door, then went up the two steps.

Inside, it was bright and smelled like tuna fish.

My stomach stopped grumbling. I was tired of eating tuna. When I moved to Paris, I'd never eat it again. Flaky croissants and buttered baguettes for me!

Hunched over her laptop at the kitchen table, Georgia barely glanced up at us. "Hey, family." She was probably looking for school scholarships or reading about the University of Vermont—her two obsessions. "I made tuna salad for sandwiches."

"Thanks, sweetheart." Mom kissed the top of Georgia's head. "I'll be out to eat after a quick shower. I smell gross."

Mom did smell a lot like house cleaner. Dad used to smell faintly of motor oil when he came home from work. I missed that smell.

"Okay," Georgia mumbled to her computer screen.

Miss Genevieve greeted me by sniffing around my feet and giving my ankle a quick lick. I reached down and patted his soft head, then threw my bag onto the bench seat across from Georgia so I could pet my pooch properly. After a scratch on the rump, which made Miss Genevieve wiggle his stubby tail and look up at me with his lovely, big eyes, I whispered, "You're the best dog on the planet, Miss Genevieve. You're even better than Scarlett Bananas, but don't you dare tell her I said that."

"You should really call him Roscoe. You're confusing him. Dogs' brains aren't that big."

"Miss Genevieve's brain is!" I gave him an extra scratch under his velvety ears. "It's filled with love and joy." When we got Roscoe from the shelter, I suggested changing his name to Miss Genevieve because that was

63

the dog's name from *Madeline's Rescue* and I loved that dog, but I was overruled by my family. So I kept calling him Miss Genevieve because Roscoe is a boring name that someone at the shelter probably picked without giving it any thought.

"Love and joy," Georgia said. "Wish I were a dog."

"Me too." I plopped across the table from Georgia and pushed the bag with my ballet clothes farther away. I didn't want them near me. Looking at my sister, I wished my hair were full and curly and dark like hers, even though she complained and said it was a frizzy mess. Her hair would probably look great in a bun.

Georgia peered over the top of her computer. "What, Cleveland?"

"Nothing." Miss Genevieve sat near his food bowl and looked up at me. "Did you feed him?"

Georgia shook her head, as if showing off her gorgeous mane of hair. "Of course I fed Roscoe."

"Thanks." My job was taking care of Miss Genevieve, but Georgia helped sometimes. Dad used to walk Miss Genevieve every morning and feed him breakfast. That was "before."

Life got divided into "before" and "after" that awful day on May 12 when Dad was arrested for stealing money from Mr. Ronnie Baker.

That day, I was at the kitchen table like I was now, except Georgia wasn't there. I was doing my homework about the life cycle of a plant. Someone pounded on the door and shouted, "Police! Open up!" which scared the snot out of me. Miss Genevieve barked his head off. Dad had just gotten out of the shower. He was wearing jean shorts, his T-shirt with the alligator lying on a lounge chair under a palm tree and sipping a grown-up drink with a tiny umbrella in it, and his flip-flops. His hair was damp.

He nudged Miss Genevieve out of the way with his foot and opened the door.

A police officer asked Dad his name, then grabbed my dad—*my dad!*—turned him around, and snapped handcuffs onto his wrists.

One of Dad's flip-flops fell off, but the officer let him put it back on.

I got a glimpse of Dad's terrified eyes, which scared me more than anything.

My heart pounded. I was rooted to my seat and couldn't do anything but clutch my pen with trembling fingers. I wished Mom and Georgia weren't at the store. "Daddy, what's happening?" I whimpered.

He looked back at me, his mouth open, but no words came out.

Miss Genevieve barked and barked.

I had to do something. Finally I stood and yelled, "Get off him!"

"You'd better get your dog, girl," the officer said to me.

"It's okay, Roscoe," Dad said in a choked voice.

It wasn't okay. Nothing was okay.

"Let my dad go!"

"Relax," the officer said. "We're not hurting him."

"It's okay, Cleveland."

But Dad's voice told me it was anything but okay. What was happening?

Miss Genevieve barked again.

"I'm warning you," the officer said to me.

That was when I noticed the gun on his holster and grabbed Miss Genevieve by his collar. I petted his head while watching the police take my dad out of our home. "It's going to be all right," I said more to myself than him. "It's going to be all right," I lied.

Then I left Miss Genevieve inside and shut the door so he couldn't get out. He kept barking through the closed door. I hoped the officer wouldn't get mad because I couldn't stop him from barking.

The officer walked Dad to a police car as Mom and Georgia pulled up.

That was when I noticed another police officer. And another police car. Why? What did they think my dad did? *This is a mistake,* I wanted to scream. *Let my dad go!*

Mom leaped out of our car, followed by Georgia.

Relief flooded through me, because Mom and Georgia were finally here and would fix everything.

"What's happening?" Mom's eyes were wild as she ran up to the officer who was holding Dad. "What are you doing with him?" Then she looked at my dad and said his name in the saddest voice I'd ever heard. "John?"

Dad started crying.

The only other times I'd ever seen my dad cry were when he told us his sister, my aunt Annette, had died suddenly of a heart attack, and more recently, when the vet had taken X-rays of Miss Genevieve and told us that before we owned him, someone must've shot him with a BB gun, because he still had a BB lodged in his stomach. I understood why Dad cried then. But why was Dad crying now? Had he actually done something wrong? Georgia pressed next to me and squeezed my hand so hard I had bruises the next day. She had her other hand over her mouth.

Do something! I wanted to shout at her.

Neighbors stood outside their trailers now, watching. Ms. Welch wore slippers and clutched her flowered bathrobe closed.

Why weren't they doing anything? Somebody needed to help my dad!

The officer read Dad his rights as he shoved him into the back of his police car.

"John!" Mom shrieked. She reached out with one shaky hand that hung there in the humid air.

But it didn't matter.

None of it mattered.

Dad was in the back of a police car, and all he could do was look at us with a world's worth of sorry in his teary eyes. Before he looked down.

Georgia let go of my hand and ran over to Mom, held her up because she was wobbling.

"Wha-what's happening?" Mom muttered.

Georgia squeezed her tighter. I pressed my body close to Georgia.

The neighbors were whispering behind their hands and watching us as though what was happening to our family was some sort of reality TV show. I wanted to punch each one of them right in the face to make them stop looking at us like that.

I was glad when Georgia tugged on my sleeve and pulled me toward the trailer. "Come on, Cleve," she said in a soft voice.

The three of us went inside, where Miss Genevieve was still barking.

Georgia and I bent to pet him. Mom paced the small

space in our trailer, tapping her chin, like she was trying to figure out some kind of complicated puzzle.

Even though we were inside, I still felt the neighbors' judgmental stares on my skin. I had a feeling they were continuing to peek out their windows as we left for the police station to find out what was going on with Dad.

I had thought the day the police came and took my dad was the worst day, but I was wrong. It turned out the real worst day came five weeks later, when Dad and his lawyer did something called a plea bargain, and Dad got seven months of jail time at Wayside. *Seven months!* Just for stealing a couple hundred dollars from Mr. Baker's auto supply shop. I understood Dad shouldn't have done that—of course stealing was wrong—but seven months in jail for a couple hundred dollars didn't seem fair. Maybe he could have been required to work and pay it back, or even pay it back double or triple. But seven months of jail was such a long time to be away from everything you loved.

Those bad days happened before Dad stole my money. And it was a *lot* more than he took from Mr. Baker. When Dad stole my money right before he went to jail, he also took my dreams. My trust. *How can I ever believe in my dad again?*

And yet, it was hard to stay angry with him for what he did, because I kept feeling sad. Sad that he was stuck in such an awful, scary place. Sad that Mom and Georgia had to work so many more hours. Sad because I was lonely and missed him.

I rubbed Miss Genevieve's silky ear. *Do you miss Dad too? I wish we could take you to the video visitation center. Everyone would love you there, especially Dad. I bet he misses the heck out of you, sweet boy.*

Georgia tapped the top of her computer with a pen. "Did you know they offer weirdly specific scholarships?"

I shook thoughts of Dad from my mind, but the sadness lingered. The paper bag beside me reminded me of what had happened at Miss Delilah's school today. "Do they have scholarships for lousy dancers from Sassafras who want to go to Paris?"

Georgia squinted at me, like she was trying to figure something out. "You have to hear some of these, Cleve." She pulled her hair back into a wild ponytail, dark curly strands pointing in every direction. Maybe Georgia's hair could never be corralled into a perfect ballerina bun. "They have scholarships for people who want to be clowns, for people who are natural redheads, and for left-handed people. But here's the best one: the National Potato Council gives away a ten-thousand-dollar scholarship to a graduate student who is studying something to benefit the potato industry."

"Maybe you should study potatoes," I offered helpfully.

Georgia put her hands flat on the table on either side of the computer. "Maybe I should. Why is it so hard to find money for college when it seems like so much is available?"

I bit my bottom lip. The reason Georgia needed money for college next year was because Mom had to spend the money they'd saved toward my sister's college tuition to pay for Dad's bail and his lawyer. Mom explained that things would have been much worse for Dad if they didn't hire their own lawyer. Georgia was applying for academic scholarships through the University of Vermont, plus private scholarships wherever she could find them. Her deadline was fast approaching: January 15. I knew that because Georgia had written the date on a sticky note, circled it with red pen, added a few hearts, and stuck it on the fridge.

I wanted to say something to make her happy. "Mom got your money back from Miss Delilah."

Georgia tilted her head. "Why would Mom—"

"I got kicked out."

"Wh–what?"

I nodded, because if I tried to talk, I might cry again. Too much had happened today, plus I was tired.

Georgia closed her computer and pushed it out of the way. "Oh, Cleve, what happened?"

There was so much kindness in Georgia's voice. A few hiccup-y sobs erupted. It felt good to let them out, but I was glad Mom was in the shower so she couldn't hear me; she had enough things to deal with, like having to clean fancy people's toilets all day instead of traveling to cool places around the world, like she wanted to.

"Cleveland?" Georgia asked gently.

"Those girls . . . those girls . . ." My words got stuck after that.

Georgia stood and scooted next to me on the bench. She wrapped her arm around my shoulders and said in a fierce voice, "You're better than those girls, Cleveland Potts." Resting her chin on top of my beret, she whispered, "Way better."

Hiccup. "Thanks, George." *Hiccup.*

My sister knew when I needed extra love.

I told her everything. Even the part where the girls laughed about Dad and made me so angry and, if I'm being totally honest, embarrassed. It was the same feeling I had when the neighbors came out to stare when Dad was put into that police car. The feeling that made my cheeks burn and my eyes look downward. The feeling I got when Mom and I walked through the market

72

and some women would mumble about us as soon as we passed and I'd see Mom's grip tighten on the handle of our shopping cart. The feeling I was sure Georgia got right after Dad was sentenced and a customer in her checkout line told her he'd read about our dad in the newspaper, then glared at her like it was Georgia's fault.

Shame.

The Best Way to Say Sorry

GEORGIA MARCHED TO OUR FREEZER and returned with an ice-cream sandwich. "This situation calls for way more than a tuna-salad sandwich, Cleve. You need dessert."

A laugh bubbled out of me. I ate the whole ice-cream sandwich, while Miss Genevieve snuffled at my feet, probably hoping I'd drop a piece for him. But chocolate wasn't good for dogs, so he didn't get any. Plus, I was super hungry and the ice cream tasted so good.

Georgia poked him with her toe. "No ice-cream sandwiches for you, Mr. Roscoe." She dropped a few pieces of kibble into his bowl, though. "Come get a treat, buddy."

Georgia, I realized, was always feeding everybody.

After my real dinner of tuna-salad sandwiches and sliced oranges, I cleaned up the few plates so Georgia could keep searching for scholarships. "They have a scholarship for high school seniors who participate in a duck-calling competition," she said.

"Duck!" Mom yelled.

This for some reason made Georgia and me bend down low, as though something was going to hit us in our heads.

Mom cracked up. She had a high-pitched laugh that startled you when you first heard it and always made Miss Genevieve bark.

Miss Genevieve's barking made me laugh, and then Georgia lost it, and somehow, we all ended up laughing so hard, we were wiping tears from our eyes.

When Mom came up for breath, she said, "I love you girls so much. You know that. Right?"

"All for one!" Georgia yelled.

"And one for all!" I replied.

Me and Mom raised our arms in solidarity.

It was really hard without Dad sometimes, but other times it was nice being just the three of us and Miss Genevieve. I wondered what it would be like when Dad came back home. One thing I knew for sure: I was going to find a better way to hide the money I earned from my dog-walking business. No way was I leaving that much cash unprotected around him again.

Better safe than sorry. *Mieux vaut prévenir que guérir.*

"It's been quite a day," Mom said. "I'm zonked. Off to bed for me." She grabbed a couple of travel magazines that she'd bought at last year's library sale. (Magazines were ten for a dollar and books were twenty-five to fifty cents each, even hardbacks, so that was when we always stocked up on reading material for the year. Mom got travel magazines, especially *National Geographic* and *Condé Nast Traveler.* Georgia looked for books of essays by women writers and poetry collections. I searched for graphic novels, books about animals, everything I could find about France, and cool cookbooks for Declan. He got more excited about a new cookbook than Miss Genevieve got about a new bone. And Miss Genevieve got pretty excited about his bones.)

After Mom went into her room with Miss Genevieve, Georgia leaned toward me. "She looks exhausted."

I worried it was my fault for making Mom leave work to deal with my problem at the dance school. "She does," I admitted. What I didn't say was that Georgia had dark circles under her eyes and looked exhausted too.

Georgia and I headed into our bedroom, which had twin beds across from each other and not much else. There wasn't space for much more. Most of the stuff we needed went under our beds or in the set of plastic drawers Mom had bought for us at the Target in Winter Beach. I didn't have many clothes—just some shorts and T-shirts mostly, so one whole drawer of mine was filled with books, comics, magazines, my tiny Eiffel Tower pencil erasers, and fourteen shiny postcards from Declan. It was my favorite drawer.

Georgia sat up in bed, with her computer on her lap. "Don't worry about those girls today, Cleveland."

"I won't." But I *was* thinking about them and what happened, remembering Jenna Finch's purple eggplant toe and feeling rotten about it. I hadn't meant to trip her. Jenna would have a perfectly normal-looking toe right now if I hadn't been in that class.

"Really, Cleve. Don't."

"I *won't*," I lied.

"They're not worth your time."

"I know." But something about all this was bothering me. Something was missing.

Georgia snapped her computer closed and put it in a box under her bed. "Tomorrow's a new day," she said in a tired voice.

My heart gave a squeeze. Dad used to say that to us if we were feeling down. *Tomorrow's a new day.*

It was supposed to make us feel better, more hopeful. Right now, it made me miss him. I could hardly remember the sound of his voice when he said it.

I peeked over and saw that Georgia was sleep-reading—that was when she kept trying to read even after her eyelids fluttered closed. The book in her hands teetered toward falling onto her face. It was funny to watch. Finally the book plopped onto her chin—luckily, it was a paperback, so it didn't hit her with too much force. Georgia startled, pushed the book away, and rolled over. She'd have to find her place again tomorrow. This happened every night. I couldn't understand why she didn't put the book on the little table between our beds with a bookmark in it and go to sleep. One day a hefty hardback would smash her right in the nose. Books could be dangerous like that.

I turned off the lamp on the table between our beds and switched on the book light Declan gave me last year for my birthday. I grabbed my notebook and a pink pen from the table. I thought Jenna might like pink since it matched her duffel bag.

Then I proceeded to write a really nice sorry note to Jenna, because the more I thought about it, the more I realized it *was* my fault. I was sure Jenna's purple toe hurt like a son of a snickerdoodle right now. I wanted to feel what Jenna might be feeling. I pressed my pinkie toe into the wall, but it didn't hurt at all, so I banged it a little, but I didn't want to make noise and wake Mom or Georgia. I guessed I'd have to imagine what Jenna was going through tonight. I figured she was having trouble falling asleep because of the pain and being mad at me. I didn't blame her. I'd be mad at me too. I only wanted to get some culture and a little closer to being able to go to Paris.

I pulled the blanket tighter under my chin and listened to the frogs croaking outside. Nothing had been the same since Dad went to jail. My old friends weren't my friends anymore, and I was upset that Jenna's mom had spoken to me like I was evil. No one deserved to be talked to like that, even if they did accidentally hurt someone's toe pretty badly and made it a very unattractive shade of purple.

I was hurting too, even if no one could see it from the outside.

I also wrote the note to prove Jenna's mom wrong. Even though my dad was in jail, I still tried to do the right thing. Just because my dad had a gambling problem didn't mean I would. Just because he stole money from people he cared about didn't mean I would.

There was no way I'd ever do something like that.

I reread what I'd written to make sure it was good enough to give Jenna Finch tomorrow at school.

> *Hi Jenna,*
>
> *I'm really sorry about what happened in dance class. I didn't mean to trip you and make your toe bang into the barre so hard. It must hurt so much.*
>
> *I'm really sorry. Did I say that already? I am!* 😊
>
> *I hope your toe isn't broken, but if it is, I hope it gets better fast.*
>
> *My mom told me it takes about seven weeks for a broken toe to get better. I know that sounds like a long time, but I bet it will go quick. And you can ask people to bring you things, like Pop-Tarts and Oreos. Pop-Tarts are my favorite (as you know), especially the strawberry ones with frosting. I promise to give you a Pop-Tart to go with this note. I hope it will help you feel better, Jenna.*
>
> *Also, I hope you become a ballerina when you grow up. You already look like one.*

I was going to write something about her perfect ballerina bun, but the way Mom had talked about ballerinas and their buns, I decided to leave that out.

Once I finished, I couldn't decide how to sign it. Jenna and I used to be best friends, but now she barely acknowledged I existed. "Your acquaintance, Cleveland" didn't sound very nice.

I reached for the French dictionary I kept on our crowded bedside table. I liked to look through it sometimes when I needed a special word. This was one of those moments. As usual, my French dictionary didn't fail me. I found the perfect signature.

Cordialement,
Cleveland

That Didn't Go Well

N THE MORNING THE FIRST thought that floated through my mind was, *Tomorrow's a new day.* Those words were supposed to fill me with hope and happiness, but instead a wave of sadness washed over me. I thought of how much more time Dad had in jail; he wouldn't get released for five more months and several days. That meant he'd miss all the good holidays, except Valentine's Day. At least he'd be home in time for that one. Mom and Dad were totally mushy on Valentine's Day.

What was he thinking when he woke up this morning? Every day must feel the same to him—waking in a horrible place that wasn't his home, without Miss Genevieve curled up by his feet. There must be scary sounds in jail instead of nice frogs croaking outside. Did they have ice cream in jail? Was he allowed to watch *Jeopardy!*, his favorite TV show? Dad and Mom couldn't dance in the kitchen, like they sometimes did when they were in good moods or when Dad won money at the dog park. Ugh.

Why did he love that dog park so much? Why did he steal that money? I knew Dad thought he'd win it all back and more. That was what he'd told us. But that wasn't a good enough reason.

Gambling was so stupid!

I sat up and breathed my way to a calmer heartbeat. I definitely didn't want to start this new day off by crying. I needed to think about something else.

I touched the note I'd written for Jenna, and that made me feel better. I'd give it to her in math class— our first class of the day together.

Since Mom was in our bathroom, I used the time to search for a Pop-Tart to give Jenna, like I'd promised in my note. Miss Genevieve was nearby, looking up at me with those big eyes. "I'll feed you in a minute."

There was only a single Pop-Tart left in an opened silver-foil package in the box in our cabinet. And it wasn't even strawberry. I wondered if Georgia had grabbed the other one when she left for school this morning. There was no way a single Pop-Tart in an opened wrapper would be good enough for Jenna Finch.

Why didn't we have a sealed double pack of iced strawberry Pop-Tarts? That would have been perfect. I still had to walk Miss Genevieve and get ready for school, so I didn't have time to rewrite the note and take out the Pop-Tart part. I wished Mom would get out of the bathroom already. I just knew Jenna had lots of bathrooms in her fancy house and never had to wait.

I put our boring unfrosted blueberry Pop-Tart into the front pocket of my backpack and silently prayed it didn't get too squished on my walk to school.

Mom rushed out of the bathroom, tucking the MARVELOUS MAIDS AT YOUR SERVICE T-shirt into her jeans. "Cleve, I'm going to be home late today. Got an extra job for a once-a-week cleaning at a house in the fancy part of town."

Maybe it's Jenna Finch's house. "Good morning to you, too," I said.

"Good morning, baby girl." She kissed me on the forehead. "Have a nice day at school. Don't give another thought to what happened at dance yesterday. That Finch girl will be fine. You hear me?"

I nodded, thinking of the note and Pop-Tart I planned to give Jenna. Maybe she'd like my peace offering so much we'd end up being friends again. She might even ask me to sit with her at lunch and share a piece of the Pop-Tart with me, and I could bring her things so she wouldn't have to hobble around with her eggplant toe. As Dad sometimes said, *This might have been a blessing in disguise.*

I felt hopeful.

Mom grabbed the bagged lunch Georgia had made for her and left.

"Just you and me now." Miss Genevieve looked at me with the brown patch around his right eye and wagged his stubby tail. "You don't like the name Roscoe, do you, boy?" He wagged harder. "Knew it." I wished I had time to visit Declan before school. He'd probably have a two-pack of strawberry iced Pop-Tarts that I could bring to Jenna.

But sometimes you've got to go with what you've got.

When Jenna hobbled into math class surrounded by her friends, I gasped.

She was wearing pink flip-flops with plastic flamingos on top. They were really cute. I wanted a pair. The ones I had at home cost fifty cents from the Goodwill store and cut into the space between my toes, so I mostly wore my sneakers with the holes near the pinkie toes or no shoes at all.

We weren't allowed to wear flip-flops to school, but I was sure Jenna's mom got her a special exception due to her eggplant toe. There was white tape wrapped around Jenna's pinkie toe and the toe next to it. An ugly greenish-brown bruise had blossomed on the top part of her foot.

I squeezed the note into my sweaty palm. It felt so light, like it wasn't nearly enough to make up for how bad her foot looked, even with the bonus Pop-Tart. I wondered what else I could give her. I had a used scented eraser in my backpack, but she'd only like something new.

Jenna slipped into her seat, next to mine. Before I lost my nerve, I handed her the slightly sweaty note and the open Pop-Tart package. "Sorry it got a little squished in my backpack," I whispered.

Mr. Milot, our math teacher, tapped the keys of his computer at his desk while quickly glancing up and back down, most likely taking attendance. Or playing some Internet math game.

Jenna's lips moved as she read my note.

My heart hammered. *Please let it be enough.*

She peeked into the pouch, where I knew the Pop-Tart was probably a crumbled mess.

Jenna's face twisted, like she was looking into a pouch of poop.

Sorry. It's all we had.

She stood, hobbled to the front of the room in her flamingo flip-flops, and dropped both my note with the pretty pink ink and the blueberry Pop-Tart into the trash can, then returned to her desk. She pulled out some antibacterial liquid in a tiny container and rubbed a squirt of it all over her hands, as though my offering had been coated in germs.

I bit my bottom lip and stared straight ahead. I would not let her know how much that hurt.

In a fake sweet voice, Jenna said, "Thanks so much, Cleveland."

Guess we wouldn't be eating lunch together anytime soon.

Then, in a quieter voice, almost to herself: "I don't know why I was *ever* friends with you."

Her words were a punch to the gut, but I wouldn't look at her. Wouldn't cry. All I'd done was try to say sorry. Why were people mean to me when things were already so hard?

My breathing came in short bursts through flaring nostrils.

Mr. Milot grabbed a stack of papers and stood. "Ready?"

Some students groaned at the quizzes about to land on their desks.

I wanted to groan too, but for a different reason.

I wished I were somewhere else—not sitting next to awful Jenna Finch in miserable middle school in stupid Sassafras, Florida. I wanted to be wearing a neat uniform with a pleated skirt and matching jacket with a school patch sewn onto the pocket and sitting at my desk at the American School of Paris, where students were cultured. No one would have such bad manners to make someone feel rotten for writing a sorry note and giving a peace offering, even if it was a little squished. And they definitely wouldn't be mean to an old friend, especially when her dad was in jail.

"Clear your desks, please."

Formidable! Wonderful! (Math quizzes seemed a good time for French sarcasm.)

My stomach erupted with an embarrassing noise. I could feel people staring at me. I was hungry. That Pop-Tart would have tasted good. Sometimes the squished ones seemed to taste better.

As I waited for the math quiz, I wondered if they sold strawberry Pop-Tarts with icing in Paris. I was pretty sure they did, but there might be so much other good stuff to eat, like chocolate-filled croissants and buttery, lemon-flecked layer cakes and madeleines, that I might not even want to eat a lowly Pop-Tart there.

I glanced over at Jenna.

She tapped her flip-flopped foot and winced.

Good! I'm glad it hurts!

But then I remembered when Miss Genevieve had a thorn in the pad of his paw. He snapped at me when I tried to pull it out. Sweet Miss Genevieve snapped at *me*. Pain can make you mean sometimes. Maybe Jenna's pain was terrible, horrible, the worst ever. Maybe I should cut her some slack. Maybe she'd be nicer to me after her toe got better, like she used to be.

Mr. Milot dropped a math quiz onto my desk and rapped on the surface with his knuckles. "Eyes front, Cleveland."

"Sorry." As I examined the quiz on my desk, only one thought ran through my mind (in two languages, of course).

I have problems! *J'ai des problèmes!*

I sneaked a peek at Jenna. She was scribbling fiercely, like she was built to get an A on this quiz.

I tugged down the sides of my beret, wishing I could hide inside it until the end of, oh, seventh grade.

C'est la vie.

Visiting Day

"Y OU READY TO ROLL, CLEVELAND?" Mom called
from the bathroom.

I leaned on the wall and slipped on my
sneakers.

Mom was applying makeup to her eyelids. She
never wore makeup, except on visiting Sundays. She
also wasn't wearing her MARVELOUS MAIDS AT YOUR
SERVICE T-shirt today. Instead she wore a pretty blue
shirt with jeans and a nice pair of flats. You had to
be careful what you wore on visiting day. Your clothes
had to be "appropriate." Mom had read me the rules.
Shoulders had to be covered. No short-shorts. No
plunging necklines. I thought those things were kind

of silly, because we were only seeing Dad on a video screen.

"Let's go, Cleve!" Mom wore pink lipstick that made her lips shimmer.

I shuffled out behind her to our car, wondering if I should have worn lip gloss or something fancier. My shorts and T-shirt didn't seem nice compared to what Mom wore.

The drive to the town of Babcock Lakes took for-ev-er, and it was so hot with our broken air conditioner (another nonessential, according to Mom) that I felt sick to my stomach. Mom had a plastic spray bottle in the car, so we could spritz ourselves with water, but that just made me slightly damp as well as unbearably hot.

Mom reached over and patted my knee. "We'll go out for a treat on the way home. Ice cream. Cold, cold ice cream."

I hoped there was room in my stomach for ice cream with the big boulder currently taking up so much space in there. "Sounds good."

Mom maneuvered Miss Lola Lemon into a parking spot at the video visitation center, between a junker and a late-model Chevy.

"I guess we're here." Mom pulled down her visor and checked her face in the mirror.

"You look perfect." She really did look pretty, but Mom looked good without makeup.

"Thanks, Cleve." She licked her lips. "I'm a little nervous."

"Nervous? You? Why?"

Mom closed the visor and looked at me. "I don't like coming here."

"Really? Me neither." It felt good to admit that.

Mom reached across and gave me a hug over the parking brake. Even though it made me hotter, it also made me feel better. "I'm glad you're here with me," Mom said. "It really helps."

I hadn't thought about Mom wanting me with her so she didn't have to do this alone. I'd only been thinking about how difficult it was for me.

"Team Potts!" I held my palm up for a high five.

Mom high-fived me hard. "Team Potts! I can't wait till the fourth member of our team comes home where he belongs."

"Fifth member of our team," I said. "Miss Genevieve counts."

Mom nodded. "Roscoe definitely counts. Now, let's get out of this hot car before my makeup melts right off my face."

Mom got out and started to close her car door behind

her, completely forgetting I had to come out her side. I guess Mom *was* nervous.

"Oh my gosh, Cleveland. I'm sorry."

"You sure you want me here with you?"

We both laughed, but it was more from nerves.

The video visitation center had bright ceramic artwork on the outside wall, but it didn't fool anybody. This wasn't a happy place. Nobody wanted to be here.

Mom and I walked over to the rows of wooden benches lined up outside the visitation center door.

There were so many people already waiting. Some of the women waved their hands in front of their faces, as though that would cool them off. The sheriffs could at least let us wait inside, where there was air-conditioning.

Mom wiped her palms on her jeans again and again. Seeing Mom nervous made my stomach tighten around the boulder. I couldn't blame her. There were so many locked doors and uniformed sheriffs. And that was just to see your loved ones through a video monitor. The people we "visited" were in an entirely different building somewhere else. I didn't understand why we couldn't visit Dad in person. It wasn't like he would do anything other than talk to us and maybe give me a hug.

The lady on the other side of Mom said, "I heard the

county south of us has a different way to visit. You could visit on video from your own computer. At home!"

"Really?" Mom asked. "That sounds better."

"Yes," the woman said. "Wouldn't that be nice instead of driving all the way here?"

"It would," Mom agreed. "Think of all the money you'd save on gas. And if it was someone's birthday or something special, your husband could feel like they were there too." Mom wiped her palms on her thighs. "Or whoever you're visiting."

"Exactly," the woman said. "They could feel like they're not missing so much at home." The woman looked down, then talked to her lap. "I'm visiting my son."

I recognized that dropped gaze. Shame.

"I'm sorry." Mom patted the woman's shoulder. "We're visiting my husband, Cleveland's dad."

The woman nodded at me, and then she and Mom were quiet.

I was glad because I didn't feel like talking. And I was sweating. Always sweating.

I'd probably never sweat in Paris.

An announcement came over the PA system: "Please line up for visitation. Form one line outside the main door and wait for instructions." The announcement

94

was repeated in Spanish. But not in French or any other language.

Mom patted my hand. "Let's get in there, Cleve."

Everyone around us got up and formed a line outside the glass doors. An older lady went into the nearby bathroom. A man waited outside for her. He wore a straw hat. I wondered if that hat was on the list of clothing that was permitted. Then I realized I was wearing my beret and hoped that was okay. I'd worn it before, so I guessed it would be allowed. Besides, I liked that Dad could see I was wearing the present he'd given me.

The man waiting for the woman in the bathroom nodded at me.

I nodded back.

Everyone waiting out here had something in common. When we were out in the world, people might not know we had a loved one in jail. But in the waiting area, we were all here for the same reason. The nice thing was nobody judged anyone, because we understood what it felt like.

A sheriff with a gray mustache unlocked the glass door, and people funneled into the building. When I approached the door, I stood behind it and held it open for the people following me. Every single person who walked through thanked me. Every one. That didn't happen all the time when I held the door for people at school or in town.

"Come on, Cleveland," Mom scolded.

Maybe I was holding the door for everyone to delay visiting Dad. It really did hurt to see him in there.

Mom waited in the foyer before a second glass door. The sheriff with the mustache stood beside her, holding that door open.

"Hurry." Mom motioned with her hand.

I rushed to Mom. "Sorry." I should have been more thoughtful and stayed beside her.

Inside the main room were three rows of video monitors, the screens black mirrors, and a wall with a big window, behind which a couple more sheriff deputies stood, pacing and watching. I wouldn't want that boring job.

Mom had to show her ID and a copy of my birth certificate, and then a sheriff with a ponytail checked to make sure our video visitation appointment with Dad was on the list. "You're at computer number fourteen."

Mom sat on the chair in front of the screen, inhaled deeply, and brushed her palms on her pants. I wouldn't have been surprised if there were holes forming in them by now. I stood behind her. There wasn't much room or any privacy. We were sandwiched between other computers and other people sitting in front of them.

I saw another kid about my age with his mom. I wondered if his parent was in for more or less time than Dad. Then I thought about how cruel it was to keep kids away from their parents. How was I supposed to go seven whole months without a hug from my dad? In-person visits would be better than video visits. Mom explained that this system was created because they were trying to keep people from sneaking things in. Whatever! It was flat-out cruel. What if a kid had only one parent and that parent was in jail? Who took care of them? Who would take care of me if something happened to Mom? Probably Georgia; she was old enough, but she had other things to do, like prepare for the University of Vermont next fall. I realized things could be a lot worse, but being this close to Dad and not being able to hug him or have him come home with us at the end was miserable. And because we only saw him on a screen for such a short time, I couldn't work out the parts where I was still so angry with him for taking my money and breaking my trust. It was all terrible.

"Are you sure you don't want to sit?" Mom reached up and grabbed my hand.

I squeezed back. "I'm okay here."

The ponytail sheriff rattled off a bunch of directions about what we could and couldn't do during our video visit, and then the screen turned on. We were looking at a room with an empty chair. A large timer on the wall in front of us started to count down. We were allowed a one-hour video visit twice a week, but we were only able to come on Sundays. And then, only when Miss Lola Lemon decided to run. Mom was her saddest self when our car wasn't working and she couldn't fix it in time for our Sunday visit. She tried to come every single week with either me or Georgia, depending on my sister's work schedule. She might not have liked what Dad had done, but she sure loved him.

Before all this . . . they'd always hold hands when they went out somewhere and would be sure to kiss each other goodbye before heading to work, no matter how late they were running. Before Dad's gambling took hold and went from an occasional hobby to a desperate obsession, my parents were grossly affectionate with each other. I kind of missed it.

"That timer makes me nervous," Mom said quietly.

"They shouldn't start it until Dad's already there," I whispered into her hair. "It isn't fair."

Mom nodded.

Then there he was.

My dad.

Walking into the room on the screen. He wore an embarrassing orange jumpsuit, but it was him inside of it.

Mom made a little noise when Dad walked through the door.

I might have made a little gasp too.

Dad's hair was darker than I remembered and kind of greasy. His face looked thinner than the last time I visited two weeks ago. Mom had told me the food probably wasn't very good, and we'd fatten Dad up as soon as he got home. The boulder in my stomach grew. I wished Mom hadn't made me come today.

But I liked the idea of fattening Dad up when he got home. Spaghetti. I'd cook that thick spaghetti Dad liked and ask Declan to make a batch of his delicious red sauce with roasted tomatoes, fresh basil, olive oil, and garlic. Georgia could make her yummy toasted garlic rolls, and we'd create a big salad, too. Dad used to like salad a lot. Maybe we'd even pick up a peach pie from Pamela's Pancake House. And Georgia could get whipped cream from Weezie's Market to squirt on top of the pie.

It would be the perfect welcome-home dinner.

When Dad sat in the chair and looked up at Mom and me, his whole face lit up. His smile was so wide and

99

his eyes looked so happy they almost looked sad.

"Glory." Dad said Mom's name like a prayer. His voice sounded gravelly, like he hadn't used it in a while. "You look so . . . beautiful, baby."

Mom ducked her head.

"And is that Miss Cleveland Rosebud Potts behind you? Come up closer to the screen, sweetie, so I can see you better."

I'd been determined to stay in the background, thinking maybe it wouldn't hurt so much if I was farther away. But Dad's voice melted through my resolve. I scooted next to Mom, and somehow we managed to squeeze onto the one chair, our arms pressed against each other's, which wasn't uncomfortable now because there was plenty of air-conditioning.

Mom reached her fingers out to touch the screen. "How are you, John?"

Dad put his hand up too, so it was like they were touching, even though they weren't really. I was about to put my fingers up when—

"Don't touch the screen," mustache sheriff said.

Mom's hand dropped, and my heart sank down to where that boulder sat in my stomach.

"I don't need to be cleaning up these screens when you're all done here."

We were quiet until he walked away.

Dad made an annoyed face but then smiled. "Tell me what's going on. What was your week like?" He sounded hungry for information about us.

Mom tilted her head toward me. "Cleveland?"

I watched the timer on the wall ticking down. I wanted to make it stop. I needed to focus my attention on Dad, not the stupid timer.

"Um, seventh grade is good so far." *Lie.* "Nothing much happened, though." *Lie.* I was not about to waste part of our hour together telling Dad about the disaster in Miss Delilah's dance class. If he were home with us, I would have told him. If he were home, it wouldn't have happened. At least the part where everyone gave me a pity face. And laughed at me. I know, I *know* if he were home, Dad would have hugged me and told me everything would be okay. But of course none of this would ever have happened if Dad hadn't gone to jail in the first place. I sniffed a little and was glad when Mom took over the conversation.

"John, I got an extra house to clean. And it's a weekly one."

Dad squinted, like something hurt. "I'm sorry you have to work so much, Glory."

She waved at the screen. "Oh, I don't mind."

Lie.

"Really," she said. "We just can't wait for you to get out of there."

We got quiet. I could hear other people talking to their screens. Mom had forgotten the rule we had made for ourselves—don't remind Dad how much time he still had in jail.

"We're going for ice cream after this," I blurted to fill the silence. It was the exact wrong thing to say.

We got quiet again.

It was impossible to know what to say and what not to say during our measly hour together.

"Tell me what's going on with Georgia," Dad said.

Mom told Dad how Georgia was looking for scholarships and doing well at school. "She can't wait to go to Vermont, John."

"I know," he said. "I'm so glad I'll have some time with her before she goes."

That was when a few tears leaked out, and Dad quickly wiped them away.

"It'll be okay," Mom said softly. "Soon."

I wasn't sure if Mom was trying to make Dad feel better or herself. I hated to see her so sad. Dad, too.

"I'm proud of her, is all." Dad sniffed.

I looked around the room. Some people were smiling

and others were crying. This was tougher for some people than others, but it was challenging for everyone.

The hour went both slow and fast.

Slow because of the uncomfortable pauses, not knowing what to say and what not to say.

Fast because an hour a week through a video screen would never be enough time to spend with one of the most important people in your life.

When the screen went dark, Mom looked deflated.

I pressed my shoulder into hers. She leaned her head on me.

"File out, please," the ponytail sheriff said. "We have another group waiting. It's a busy day, folks."

When I stood, half my butt had fallen asleep from sharing the chair with Mom. I never imagined I'd think this, but our car would actually feel comfortable compared to sharing a single chair with Mom for an hour.

It hurt my heart to leave, because it felt like we were leaving Dad behind.

Or had Dad left us behind when he stole that money?

Sometimes it was hard to tell the difference.

There's No Escaping It

I FELT GUILTY ORDERING THE THREE-SCOOP sundae at Snazzy's Snack Shack, because it cost way more than the single dip with sprinkles I usually ordered, but Mom said, "Today calls for an extra-big treat, Cleveland. Don't you think?"

I did, plus I was hungry. My mouth watered just thinking about it, but then Mom ordered a plain single scoop of vanilla, so I felt bad all over again. She deserved a big treat too, but we couldn't afford two big treats. Maybe we should have shared the three-scoop sundae.

I noticed the cashier very carefully counting the money Mom handed him. Did he think we were trying to cheat him? A small town was not the place to be when *someone* in your family did something bad.

When we slid onto opposite sides of the table to eat, I tried to enjoy my sundae because I knew how much it cost. It was cold and delicious—exactly what I needed. But a nagging part of my mind reminded me that Dad wouldn't be able to have an ice-cream sundae at Snazzy's until he was released on February 2. That felt so far away. It was still only August.

Mom closed her eyes when she took her first bite. "Mmm."

I was glad to see her enjoy her ice cream. "Hey," I said quietly. "When Dad gets out, let's bring him here and get the Super Jumbo Sundae Surprise for him." (The "Surprise" was that they added ten cherries to the top. Ten! I knew Dad would share some of them with me.)

"Great idea, Cleve. Bet Dad will love that."

I wasn't even done with the first scoop of my sundae when the door to Snazzy's opened, and two people walked in, causing me to lose my appetite. The boulder in my stomach was back. Mom couldn't see them because they were behind her, but I dreaded the moment she did.

"What?" Mom asked.

"Nothing." I plunged my spoon into my sundae, hoping Mom wouldn't turn.

She turned.

Dad's old boss, Mr. Ronnie Baker, and his son, Todd, who was one grade ahead of me at school, were at the counter, looking at the large menu hanging on the wall. I wanted to throw something at them. My dad couldn't be here with us because of what Ronnie Baker did to him. He could have at least given my dad a second chance. He could have . . .

"Oh," Mom said, whisper-quiet.

Her cheeks flamed pink, and she swallowed so hard I heard it.

Mom probably felt like I did when the neighbors stared at us, like I felt when the girls at the dance school gave me their pity faces and my customers wouldn't let me walk their dogs anymore. I leaned forward and whispered, "Do you want to leave?"

Mom nodded.

We grabbed our ice cream cups and stood.

Mom tossed hers into the trash on the way out, even though she'd hardly eaten any of it.

I held on to my sundae and scowled at Mr. Baker and Todd.

Stop ruining things for us!

Mr. Baker was scanning the menu, but Todd turned around and looked at me. His face wasn't mean and I

THE PARIS PROJECT

didn't see anger in his eyes, but I saw something else. *It had better not be pity!*

Mr. Baker nudged Todd. "What do ya want, bud?"

Must be nice, I thought, *to have your dad here buying you anything you want.*

Todd turned back to the menu. "Um, not sure yet."

Before Mr. Baker caught sight of me, I followed Mom out the door and across the parking lot to Miss Lola Lemon.

As we drove home, Mom stared straight ahead and kept sighing. I wished I were old enough to drive, so Mom could relax in the passenger seat and get herself together. It was hard for Mom to live in Sassafras now too. It wasn't like she could pretend we were a nice normal family, because there were always reminders, like Ronnie Baker and his son going out for ice cream at the same place we went after visiting my dad.

Très gênant!

I wished Mom and I could move to Paris tomorrow. Then we'd both be rid of stupid Sassafras and live our best lives. But I knew Mom would never do that.

She'd never leave Dad behind.

Why? Why? Why?

COULDN'T IGNORE MISS GENEVIEVE'S WHINING as soon as I got home, so I gave him a quick walk. It's a good thing I did, because he needed to poop. I picked it up right away, unlike some inconsiderate people who lived in our neighborhood and thought it was okay to let their dogs poop wherever they wanted and never clean it up. *I'm looking at you, Mr. Rich!*

When Miss Genevieve and I got back to our trailer, Georgia was still at work and Mom was sipping an iced tea, staring off at absolutely nothing. "Want to play Scrabble?" I asked, even though I really wanted to go to Declan's and talk about something important. I didn't want Mom to be by herself after what happened at

Snazzy's. I knew the visitation was a lot for Mom, too. She always looked so happy before we visited Dad and so sad afterward.

"I'll let you go first so you get the double word score to start."

"Huh?" Mom turned to me. "No, I'm good, honey."

"Sure you don't want me to stay here? We could—"

"Cleve." Mom patted the bench seat beside her.

When I sat, she wrapped an arm around my shoulders and pulled me to her. "Miss Potts, it's not your job to take care of me." She pressed her head against mine. "It's my job to take care of you."

"But Dad used to help with that." *At least he did before he got so caught up with gambling.*

Mom choked on her iced tea. I'd said something wrong.

She gave me another squeeze. "Doesn't matter. I'm still the parent. You're still the kid, and I've got this till your dad comes home. You hear me?"

I shrugged.

"Do you hear me, Cleveland Rosebud Potts?" Mom had turned toward me and was peering into my eyes.

"I hear you." I tugged my beret on tighter. "You've got this. You're going to take care of me." *But who's going to take care of you?*

"Besides . . ." Mom took a quick sip of iced tea. "Aunt Allison is coming over soon, so I won't be by myself."

"That's great, Mom."

"Yes, it's nice of her to drive that far. It will be wonderful to see her."

Aunt Allison lived all the way in Carilynntown, nearly two hours away. "And you've got Miss Genevieve to keep you company until Aunt Allison gets here."

Mom held her iced-tea glass up in a toast. "I've got Roscoe."

Miss Genevieve let out a startling snore, and we both laughed. It felt good to laugh together. I'd never thought laughing with Mom would feel like a gift. I used to take those kinds of things for granted.

"Really, Cleveland. I'm good."

"If you're sure you're okay, I'm going to Declan's."

Mom patted my hand. "You have a good time with your friend, Cleve. Tell Dec and his dad I say hey."

"Will do." I kissed Mom on the cheek. She didn't smell like bleach today. She had the faint scent of makeup and something fruity. It was nice.

Miss Genevieve got a good scratch behind the ears and a few bits of kibble before I headed out.

I couldn't wait to ask Declan a question about the second item on my Paris Project list.

. . .

I practically skipped around the long horseshoe drive-way to the Maguires' trailer. The heat actually felt good today.

Before I climbed the two steps to their door, delicious smells of garlic and onions wafted out and made my mouth water. That boy was a cooking machine!

After I knocked, the door flung open. "Scout!"

Declan's smile and the happiness in his voice made my heart thump. For a moment, I felt like the luckiest person in Sassafras. "Whatcha cooking in there, Dec?"

He held open the door for me. "Why don't you come in and find out?"

Declan went to stir something in a big pot on the stove.

As soon as I sat on the bench seat at their kitchen table, he held up a wooden spoon and waved the steam toward his nose. He raised his eyebrows, which made his ears poke out even more than usual.

After tasting the dish and adding some spices, Declan looked at himself in the window of the microwave and fussed with his hair.

That was weird. "What are you doing?" I pushed my pinkie toes up toward the holes in my sneakers, but it made me think of Jenna and her broken pinkie toe, so I stopped.

Declan turned to me like I'd caught him doing something he wasn't supposed to. "Nothing," he said a little too quickly.

"O-kay." Dec never seemed to care how he looked, especially in front of me.

He grabbed the wooden spoon, dipped it into the pot again, and rushed over to me, with his other hand underneath to catch drips. "Taste this, Scout. I think I got it right this time."

The thick liquid burned the tip of my tongue but was crazy delicious, with all sorts of flavors like onions, garlic, and cilantro bursting through. "What is that?"

Declan's face changed for a moment. Something sad passed over it. "My mom's vegetarian stew recipe." He pointed to the falling-apart, handmade cookbook on the edge of the counter.

"Oh."

"Yeah." Declan shrugged.

I remembered the day Dec first showed me that cookbook.

It was the summer after third grade, fourth for him, and almost two years after he'd moved in. That day, we'd been swimming at the community pool and came back to his trailer to eat strawberry ice pops outside on the lawn chairs. I sat in his dad's chair, which even back then sank down in the middle. Declan finished his ice pop in about three bites. But I was savoring mine, a few nibbles at a time.

"My dad gave me something special for my birthday, Cleve." (He hadn't started calling me Scout back then.)

"A video game system?" I asked hopefully, because I knew if Declan got that, we'd spend the entire summer playing games together, and it would be the best summer ever. Jenna might play with us too. There weren't too many kids our age in the neighborhood besides Jenna Finch. She hadn't moved to her fancy-pants house yet. It was mostly filled with really little kids and a bunch of nosy old people. The three of us hung out together whenever Jenna's mom didn't have her scheduled for some activity. Even back then, Jenna was in dance, gymnastics, and Brownies, and had summer math tutoring twice a week, not to mention her church activities every Wednesday evening and Sunday morning.

"I'd love a game system," Dec had said. Then his face got serious. "This is better, though."

Now I was curious. My ice pop dripped on the ground as I leaned over. "What is it?" I couldn't imagine anything better than getting a video game system for your tenth birthday.

Declan bit his lip. "You know how my mom . . ."

"Yeah," I said real quick, because I didn't want Declan to have to say it again. It made me uncomfortable. A few months before, Dec had shared the full story of how his mom had left him and his dad and moved in with another cook at the restaurant where she worked. That was why Dec and his dad ended up moving to our trailer park. Anyway, it wasn't long after that when Dec's mom left him and his dad again, but this time permanently.

Declan puffed out his skinny chest. "My dad said I'm old enough to have the special cookbook she made. It would be mine to take care of."

I didn't think that was better than a video game system, but there was no way I'd say that. "Dec, that's really cool!"

He had run inside and brought out this beat-up, homemade book with all these handwritten recipes and photos that were falling out.

"Here, I'll show you a couple pages, but you'd better not touch it. Your ice pop might drip on it or something."

I held my ice pop far away from it and sat on my other hand so I didn't accidentally touch the book and mess it up. I could tell how important it was to Declan.

He ran his fingers over the cover, like it was made of gold, and showed me some of the pages, with recipes

114

in loopy script and little drawings of different kinds of food along the margins. Then Declan closed the thick book and held it to his chest. "Cleveland, I made a promise to myself."

"Yeah?"

"I'm going to make every single recipe in my mom's book."

I gulped. "That's a really big book, Declan. It might take a long time to do that."

"I know." Declan held the book tighter, but gently. "And I'm only going to count the dish if it comes out exactly right. That'll mean a lot of cooking and a lot of mistakes."

"And I'll be right beside you to eat those mistakes." Declan laughed.

I laughed too, but I knew it mattered a great deal, so I pointed my melting ice pop at him and offered some encouragement. "I know you can do this, Dec."

He bit his bottom lip and nodded.

Declan Maguire had been working on keeping that promise to himself ever since.

I figured all that cooking made Declan feel closer to his mom, who from what Dec told me, was a pretty amazing chef.

At the kitchen table, Dec held the wooden spoon

up like a magic wand. "Well, what do you think?"

"It's delicious." I wanted to say something more, something to help Declan overcome his sadness, but I couldn't think of what those words would be.

"Thanks, Scout." Declan put the cookbook into its plastic cover and slipped it into the drawer near the stove. "Tastes like hers did, I think. It's hard to remember anymore. I have only a few more recipes to get through and then I'll have done them all."

"Wow." I wanted to give Declan a hug but wasn't sure if that was the appropriate action, so I sat still and felt some of his sadness wash over me.

He went back to stirring the stew, mesmerized by it, now in a total daze. Suddenly he put the spoon down and checked his hair again in the reflection from the microwave.

Why is he doing that? "Dec?"

"Yeah?"

I decided not to ask him what all his fussing was about. "I could use your help with something." I bit the skin at the edge of my thumbnail. "It's kind of important."

Dec rushed over and sat on the bench next to me. He crossed his legs and put his chin on his hands. "Does this by any chance have to do with your Paris Project?"

Dec always got me. "Of course it does."

He nodded. "Look here, Scout. Before we go any further, I'm formally registering my protest. I don't want you to leave Sassafras. This place would stink without you. I mean, it would stink even worse than it already does."

This made me feel good. I would miss Declan, too, but I tried not to think about it. "Declan, you know you're coming with me. You'll go to that fancy cooking school, Le Cordon Bleu. Remember when we talked about that?"

Declan looked down, then back up at me. "You know how expensive that place is, right?"

"Scholarships, Dec. It's the only way I'm getting to the American School of Paris. Georgia told me there's even a big scholarship for people who want to study potatoes."

"Potatoes, huh?" He ran his hand through his hair, then patted it down.

"Of course you'll go, because we have to go to Paris together. I don't want to be over there by myself."

"Sure," Dec said. "We'll go together."

I could tell he was having second thoughts.

"I thought you couldn't wait to get out of Sassafras either."

Instead of replying, Dec grabbed his phone, glanced at the time, then looked past me, out the window.

"Waiting for something?" I thought maybe he was expecting his dad or a package to be delivered. Some new kitchen gadget he'd saved up for.

Dec didn't answer, but his fingers tapped a nervous pattern on the table. "What do you need help with?" he asked. "Test you on French words? Could we maybe do it tomorrow, Scout?"

"Tomorrow?"

"I mean—"

"No. I don't even need help with that. I'm using the library's French language CDs for that part of the plan." Which I had already told him about.

Dec popped up, stirred the stew, checked himself out in the glass of the microwave, then looked out the window again.

What in the hammock is going on? "Could you help me learn to cook a French dish?"

"French dish? Well . . ." He glanced at his phone again.

I tilted my head. *Why isn't Declan inviting me to stay for dinner?* He always asked me to stay for dinner when he cooked a big pot of something. I was pretty sure he could hear my stomach rumbling. "Dec?"

"Yeah?"

"Cooking? French dish? Help?"

"Oh yeah, I can help you with that, Scout." Declan wiped his palms on his shorts, like Mom did when she was . . . nervous. "Let's figure out a time to do that."

Declan Maguire was trying to get rid of me!

I jumped up. I knew when I wasn't wanted. *But why?*

He walked me toward the door and bounced up onto his toes a few times. "We'll definitely find a day for me to help you with that French dish. Okay?" he said in one breath.

"Okayyy," I said, not understanding what was happening.

Then Declan opened the door so I could *leave*. That was when I saw why he was rushing me out. My brain couldn't process what it was seeing. The wires in it short-circuited. This couldn't be happening twice in one day.

"Um . . . ," Declan said from beside me.

I croaked out one battered syllable: "Dec?"

In front of us stood Todd Baker, eyes wide, his mouth rounded into a tight circle. "Oh . . ."

I pushed past the boy who made me think of the single worst day of my life and stormed away from Declan's trailer, breathing hard through my nostrils.

There were not enough slow breaths in the world to make me feel better right now.

I hurried around the horseshoe-shaped driveway toward home but knew I couldn't go there. Not yet. So I stomped right out of the trailer park and angry-walked along the side of the road, overgrown with grass and weeds, all the way to town.

Why?

Why would Declan Maguire, my very best friend, invite that traitor over to his home?

Why?

Why?

Why?

Not Listening!

THE NEXT DAY AT SCHOOL, Declan approached me at my locker before classes started.

"Scout?"

Usually, hearing him call me that sent a fizzy feeling from my head down to my toes, but today it flowed through my body like molten lava. I whirled around. "Don't call me that!"

Kids turned to look at us. I didn't care. Declan Maguire was a traitor!

He opened his mouth but then closed it again. His teeth were kind of yellow.

"And don't talk to me!" I slammed my locker door to emphasize my words, but one of my books was sticking out, so the door bounced open, and Declan laughed a little.

I looked right in his face. "It's so not funny, Declan." But I wasn't talking about the locker door, and I might have spit in his face a little.

He stepped back and wiped off his cheek. "Scout, let me explain. Please."

Declan's voice broke on that last word. He sounded like he might cry, but I didn't care.

"No!"

I managed to close my locker and stormed off to class, where I had to sit next to Jenna Finch, who was still wearing her flamingo flip-flops, even though the bruise on her foot was almost totally cleared up. I guessed rich people didn't have to follow the same rules about proper footwear as everyone else at school. I looked down at the holes in my sneakers and got twelve kinds of angry. But I knew I wasn't mad at my falling-apart sneakers or the injustice of Jenna wearing those flamingo flip-flops.

Since Dad went to jail, it felt like every single thing had gone wrong. Not that everything was perfect before that, but it was pretty good most of the time. And now this . . . this! Declan Maguire inviting the son of the man who put my dad in jail to his home.

This was the lowest. The absolute worst. What kind of friend did that?

No kind of friend at all.

Walking around the crowded halls of school, I felt so alone, and I realized exactly why: I had no friends.

Broken

I T WAS HARD TO AVOID Declan during school days, but when I saw him in the halls, I did an about-face, even if it took me out of my way and made me late for class. It was more than two weeks since I'd seen Todd come to Declan's house. Since then, I'd spied Declan talking to Todd near his locker more than once. They'd stand close; Declan looked so happy, which made me even angrier. Out of all the people at Sassafras Middle School, Todd Baker had to be the person to make Declan smile?

It was easier to avoid Declan at home. I kept a wide radius around his house where I wouldn't allow myself to walk—alone or with the dogs. It was easier . . . and it was harder. The truth was, I missed Declan. I already had to survive without my dad. And Jenna. Mom and Georgia seemed to be working all the time. Not spending time with Declan felt like too much.

Declan should've said sorry. Maybe that was what he was going to say at my locker when I wouldn't let him talk. Maybe I should have let him say something. Maybe . . .

I sat at our kitchen table and nibbled on a blueberry Pop-Tart, remembering how I'd tried to give Jenna Finch a smooshed Pop-Tart to say sorry. That seemed like a long time ago. I hadn't done a single thing on my Paris Project list since then, not even practiced French words from the library CD, which I kept renewing and ultimately ignoring. I'd been too upset to focus, but that was exactly why I had to get it together and move forward on my goals—to create my happily ever after. The least I could do was fill out the application for the American School of Paris, like Georgia was doing for the University of Vermont.

I shoved a big piece of Pop-Tart into my mouth, even though I wasn't really hungry. I wasn't really anything.

At school Jenna was back to wearing regular shoes and walking like nothing had ever happened to her pinkie toe. She still didn't talk to me, though. Except the one time I was standing behind her in the lunch line because Georgia had given me an extra dollar to buy an ice cream at school. Jenna whirled around and yelled, "Don't stand so close to me. You'll probably step on my bad toe or something." I moved back, practically bumping into the person behind me, even though I'd never step on Jenna's bad toe. I'd wanted her to talk to me again, but not like that.

Even though I spent a dollar on an ice cream, once I got back to my lonely table, I couldn't make myself eat it and ended up throwing it in the garbage. I spent the rest of lunch in a bathroom stall, crying my eyeballs out. *Très chic!*

When the school day ended, after walking Scarlett Bananas, Miss Genevieve was the only one who had time for me, but he mostly slept and seemed interested in me only when I had a treat for him or jangled his leash for a walk.

I wished Dad were around to play Monopoly or to go swimming at the community pool or even to tell one of his bad jokes that used to make me groan in agony. He told so many jokes, but for some reason I could remember only his silly pencil joke. "Knock, knock." I poked Miss Genevieve with my toe, but he didn't stir. "Who's there?" I asked my sleeping dog. "Broken pencil," I said to myself. "Broken pencil who?" I asked no one. Miss

Genevieve made a snuffling sound in his sleep. "Never mind. There's no point." And the crowd went wild. Just kidding. There was no crowd. Just me and Miss Genevieve, who had slept through the pointless joke.

Everything felt pointless.

I thought about how many bad Dad jokes I'd missed since he went to jail almost three months ago and how many I would miss until he came home. Dad wasn't the only one being punished. Our whole family was too. I hadn't done anything wrong. This wasn't fair. *Ce n'était pas juste.*

I wished I were able to go over to Declan's house. I could always talk to him about what was going on with my dad, and he would always share his feelings with me about his mom. That was the kind of friendship we had. Used to have.

If I were at Declan's right now instead of sitting here staring at my sleeping dog, he and I would probably be watching an old Julia Child cooking video and imitating her jovial high-pitched voice. "Don't forget to dress your turkey!" Or maybe he'd be at the stove, preparing some delicious meal for us to eat, a special dish from his mom's cookbook. My stomach rumbled at the thought, so I pressed a fist into it to quiet it. No use thinking about Declan's cooking now. I'd never taste a delicious morsel he made again.

I went into my room and lay on the bed, staring at all the tiny holes in the ceiling tiles. I would've counted them but knew that would depress me even more.

It would even be okay if Declan and I were doing homework together, with our books and papers spread out over his kitchen table and limeade spritzers nearby. The only thing I had to drink now was water. And not even the fizzy kind.

I grabbed my French dictionary from the little table beside my bed and threw it at the wall across the room.

Miss Genevieve lumbered in and let out a startled bark.

"Sorry, Miss Genevieve."

I dragged myself off my bed and picked up the two halves of the book. It had split right down the middle of the spine.

My French dictionary was ruined! I'd have to find duct tape to fix it, but I didn't have the energy.

I lay back in bed, squeezing my pillow to my chest.

How could Declan and I not be friends anymore? How had this happened? I'd thought we'd be friends forever.

Maybe, like the French dictionary, I could fix this. Give Declan a chance to make it up to me.

That was what a good friend would do. Maybe this friendship with Todd was just a temporary thing, a class assignment or lab-partner homework; maybe I'd over-reacted and now things could go back to the way they had been.

I closed my eyes.

Yes. I'd definitely give Dec a chance to make it up to me.

Tomorrow.

Stay

I T TOOK ME NEARLY THREE weeks to gain the courage
to go to Declan's. Three weeks of excuses. Three
weeks of wasted time. Three weeks of cowardice. It
was already October. How could I be afraid to go to my
best friend's home?

Sitting beside Miss Genevieve on the floor, I whispered, "It's hard not having any friends."

Miss Genevieve let out a soft snore.

"I know. The longer I stay away, the harder it will be
to go over there."

And Sunday seemed as good a day as any to do it.
"Right, Miss Genevieve?"

He opened one sleepy eyelid, then closed it again.

I was annoying him.

Georgia had taken the day off from Weezie's to go to the video visitation center with Mom.

"We'll miss you, Cleve," Mom said when I told her that I felt like staying home.

This made me feel good. "I have to walk the dogs, too."

"Yes, you do."

I'd gotten three new customers for my dog-walking business, and two of them wanted me to walk their pooches on weekends, too; I was earning ninety dollars per week now. And I'd already saved $160 from walking Scarlett Bananas before the new customers called me. *Cha-ching!* Not everyone judged me because of Dad being in jail. My Paris Project fund was finally growing. I didn't have nearly as much as when Dad took everything, but it was slowly building back up. I'd have enough to get a passport and maybe pay the application fee. Plus, I loved spending time with all my dog customers. It felt so good when they'd get all waggy and excited as soon as I walked in the door. Dogs made everything better.

I finished with my four-legged customers pretty early and then prepped myself for the walk to Declan's. I knew I had to do it today or I might find excuses for the rest of my life.

Miss Genevieve made a snorfling noise and put his chin on my feet.

"That's what I'm talking about, Miss Genevieve."

He closed his eyes and let out a big breath.

"I should go over to Declan's now," I told Miss Genevieve. "There's no reason to put it off anymore."

He didn't answer.

I gently pulled my feet from under Miss Genevieve's chin and let him settle onto the floor. Then I made my bed. The bed looked good, but the rest of our room was messy, so I tidied everything up. Georgia would be pleased when she got home. After that, I cleaned the kitchen and made some Jell-O, in case Mom and Georgia wanted a snack when they came back from visiting Dad.

I couldn't think of anything else to do, because there was no way I was cleaning the bathroom, even if it would have allowed me to avoid facing Declan a little longer. I had my limits.

I pulled my shoulders back, grabbed my key, and walked all the way around the horseshoe driveway to the Maguire trailer. It was a familiar path, but it felt different today. It had been exactly thirty-five days since I'd walked it—way too long. I'd missed the entire month of September. I'd never gone that long without going to Declan's house.

You can do this, Cleveland Rosebud Potts. But I wondered if I might be lying to myself. Maybe I absolutely could not do it, like I couldn't survive one lousy day of ballet school. Perhaps there were some things I wasn't good at, things I was downright rotten at. Overcoming this giant hurdle in my friendship with Declan could be one of those things. What if I couldn't fix it? That thought made me sad.

I heard Dad's voice in my head: *Doing the right thing sometimes means doing the hard thing.*

This was the right thing. And it was definitely hard.

The lawn chairs weren't out front. Both the regular one and the sagging one were gone. For one terrible moment, I thought maybe the Maguires were gone too. It made me want to run up to the door, fling it open, and beg Declan to forgive me, even though I didn't know what I'd done wrong, other than stand by my dad, who maybe didn't exactly deserve to be stood by. I was still trying to figure out all my feelings, which was precisely why it would have been nice to have a true friend to help me do that. Thinking about this made me angry. *Why didn't Declan stick by me?* He knew how much I needed a friend. He knew hanging out with Todd Baker was probably the worst thing he could have done to me.

While I stood outside, biting my lower lip and imagining all kinds of scenarios, I realized something. There had been plenty of opportunities for Declan to come to *our* trailer and apologize to *me*, to let me know he was sorry for hurting me. But he never did. Maybe Declan was scared I'd slam the door in his face. Or maybe . . . maybe . . . Declan didn't want to be my friend anymore.

If I weren't so sick of my own company, I'd have walked right back home and spent the rest of the day inside with Miss Genevieve. But I couldn't stand being by myself (even with Miss Genevieve)—couldn't bear being without my best friend—for another minute.

So I climbed the two steps, took a couple of shaky breaths, and knocked. It wasn't my usual enthusiastic, let-me-in knock. It was so soft I almost couldn't hear it myself.

But someone must have heard, because the door swung open.

I choked on my own saliva.

Mr. Maguire stood there. His burly frame, his wiry beard and messy hair, the exact same color as Declan's, his wide smile that made the skin at the sides of his eyes crinkle.

"Darlin'!"

I held back tears. Even before my dad went to jail,

Mr. Maguire had been like a second father to me, and I didn't realize how much I needed that. *Darn you, Declan, for making things change when I didn't need any more changes.*

Mr. Maguire scratched his beard. "I haven't seen you in way too long, Miss Cleveland. How are you? How's your mom and sister?" He pulled me inside by the elbow. "Come in here, sweetheart!" Then he turned toward the kitchen table. "Look who's here, boys!"

Boys?

I turned toward the kitchen table. There were two boys sitting there.

Two.

Declan and Todd looked at me with their mouths hanging open, like I was the intruder.

There was a limeade spritzer sitting on the table in front of Todd. *That's my drink!* I clenched my fingers into fists.

Mr. Maguire clapped, startling me. "Can I get anyone a snack?"

No one answered, and then Declan scrambled up. He turned to Todd and held up a finger. "Be right back."

Where is he going? Don't leave me here with Todd Baker!

Declan raised his eyebrows at me, then led me right back out of the trailer.

There was nowhere to sit anymore. But I was way too irritated to sit anyway. I couldn't imagine what Declan could say to make this right. I wondered if I should bolt home. If I did, I knew I'd never come back.

Why, oh why, couldn't I be living in Paris right now?

Dec leaned against the trailer and looked at me with the saddest eyes I'd ever seen. Sadder than Miss Genevieve's were when we were eating dinner and wouldn't give him any scraps. Sadder than Georgia's when her first boyfriend, Marcus Kraft, took another girl to the eighth-grade dance. Sadder than Dad's the first time we saw him through the screen at the video visitation center. I didn't know someone could look that sad and not be bawling his eyeballs out.

I desperately wanted to hug Declan but crossed my arms instead.

"Cleve?"

Declan didn't use his special nickname for me.

This was terrible. *Terrible!*

Forget Julia Child videos. Forget limeade spritzers. Forget celebrating Halloween together at the end of the month, like we always did. Our friendship was over. *Fini.*

He held his hands up—his beautiful hands that were always cooking something or tasting something or handing me something to taste—he held those hands up like, *What am I supposed to do about all of this?*

I knew exactly what he was supposed to do. He should have known too. Every single thing roiling inside me exploded at him. "Of all the friends you could have picked . . ." I motioned toward the trailer. "Why him, Dec?"

Declan opened his mouth, then closed it. Opened, then closed, like a fish that was dying on a dock.

I wanted to rescue him but was filled to the brim with anger and loneliness and frustration. It was like how I felt about my dad. "Declan Maguire, you knew how much that would hurt me." I stamped my foot like I was back in second grade. "You knew!"

Then Declan did the most surprising thing.

He walked toward me, opened his arms, and enveloped me in a hug.

A hug! *Un étreinte!*

My arms were still crossed between us, but I let him hold me. His arms were warm. Safe.

"I know, Cleve. I'm sorry," he whispered.

I pulled back so I could look at him. Really look at him and make sure he was for real.

He glanced down, then back up at me, with those brown eyes that always gave away exactly how he was feeling. "I'm sorry I hurt you, Scout."

Scout. Maybe we were still friends after all.

Declan kicked at the rocks littering the ground. "But I . . . like Todd. I get, I don't know, tingly whenever I'm around him. I've never felt this way around anyone else before." He looked up, his eyes bright. "If you'd give him a chance, you'd see—"

Tingly? "His dad sent my dad to jail."

"I know." Declan ducked his head. "But your dad—"

"My dad what?" I dared him to finish.

Declan held my shoulders and looked right at me. "None of that is Todd's fault. He didn't have one single thing to do with any of it. You get that. Right?"

Declan's words hit me like a smack in the face. "But . . ." *Have I been blaming Todd for something his father did?* I remembered when Jenna's mom said I was bad like my dad. *Have I been doing the same thing to Todd?* "But even if that's true and Todd had nothing to do with any of this . . ." I was having trouble catching my breath. "Wasn't there one other person in all of Sassafras you could have picked to hang out with?"

Declan answered with one quiet sentence. "He's the best person in Sassafras."

My eyes went wide.

"Besides you, Scout. Besides you."

I didn't know whether to be happy that Declan

basically said I was one of the best people in Sassafras or angry that he thought Todd was too. So many feelings swirled inside me and made me want to jump out of my skin. "This—this—"

"It's really hard," Declan said.

In some ways Dec was like a wise old man who always understood what I was feeling. Maybe because of all he'd been through with his mom. "Yeah." I sniffed.

"I've missed hanging out with you, Scout."

A hot tear snaked down my cheek. "Oh, Dec." I looked up at the trailer and realized Declan had left Todd in there all this time so he could talk to me. "You know . . ." I swiped my cheek. "I never realized how boring Sassafras was."

We both laughed.

"It's pretty boring."

Our laughter, it sounded so good, like everything would be okay. Dec was still here, standing right in front of me. He was the same person I'd known since I was in the second grade. He was still my friend.

Nothing had changed.

The trailer door opened, and Todd Baker jogged down the steps with his perfectly styled brown hair with its weird bump at the top and his shiny baseball jersey that was too small on him.

Even if he wasn't responsible for the terrible thing his dad did to my dad, Todd had just ruined the best moment I'd ever had with Declan.

"I'd better get going," Todd said.

Yes, you should, I thought. *Go!*

Declan grabbed Todd's arm. "Don't go." Dec looked at me, then back at Todd. "Stay," he said with an intensity I hadn't heard before.

It felt like there was no room for me in that intensity.

Declan moved a half step closer to Todd but turned to me. "Both of you. Please. Stay."

Todd ran his fingers through his hair. That weird bump stuck up even worse. "Okay," he said. "Okay. I guess I can stay."

Then both boys looked over at me.

My heart thumped. Part of me wanted to stay, wanted everything to be like it was before. Another part wanted to run home and have more time to figure everything out. I gulped. "I can stay too. For a little while."

Declan pretend-punched me in the shoulder. "Thanks, Scout."

Todd tilted his head. "Scout?"

"It's from *To Kill a Mockingbird*." Dec bumped his hip into mine. "Right?"

"Right." I stood a little taller because Declan and I

had a secret between us that Todd didn't understand.

"Never read that one," Todd said.

Because you're a dummy. But I kept that thought inside my own head.

I could hardly believe it, but the three of us walked back into the Maguires' trailer.

Together.

Figuring Out Some Things

GEORGIA LAY ON HER BED across from me. The lights were off in our room, but there was plenty of soft light from the full moon. I wadded up my blanket and hugged it, like it was a stuffed toy animal. I needed comfort, and since Miss Genevieve wouldn't curl up with me in bed, I had to improvise.

"It was weird," I told her. "Being at Declan's with Todd Baker there."

Georgia filed her nails while we talked. She rarely did one thing at a time. "Weird how?"

"Well, we watched videos." I rested my chin on the balled-up blanket and thought about the word Declan had used to describe his feelings around Todd—*tingly*.

"Cooking videos. Sports blooper videos. Funny animal videos. You know, all three of us together, but Dec sat real close to Todd while we watched. He kept nudging Todd and poking him, and one time, when we watched a particularly cute baby elephant video, he laid his head on Todd's shoulder for a second. I was surprised Todd didn't punch Dec for being so annoying." I thought Georgia might say something about what a traitor Declan was for hanging out with Todd. I thought she might be mad at me for being in the same space as Todd Baker. I braced myself for her response to be laced with anger, but what she said surprised me.

"Cleveland, do you think Declan likes Todd?"

"Definitely. He likes him so much I had thought he was replacing me as his friend. How much would that stink? But I think he wants to be friends with both of us now. So that's good. Right?"

Georgia stopped filing and leaned forward. "I mean *likes*. Do you think Declan *likes* Todd?"

"Oh." I thought back to Dec and Todd sitting so close together. How Dec's cheeks turned shades of pink a bunch of times, which usually meant he was embarrassed. *Tingly.* "Oh. Oh." I thought about Craig and William at that fancy restaurant Dad took us to and how Dec kept staring at the two men the whole time.

"Oh. Oh. Oh." I leaned toward my sister. "Georgia, do you think Declan . . . likes boys? I mean, do you think there's a chance he might be . . . gay?"

"Of course he is, Cleveland."

"Of course he is?" How did Georgia know this and I didn't? Wasn't I supposed to be his best friend? I felt like an idiot. *Imbécile!*

Georgia turned toward me. "It's not like Declan can be out and proud here in Sassafras."

I swallowed a lump in my throat. *But couldn't he have been out and proud with me?* "Well, that's not fair."

"Yah think? That's one of the reasons I can't wait to move to Vermont. Ms. Douglas, our school librarian, said it was liberal and open-minded, the best place she's ever lived."

"Then why does she live here now?"

Georgia went back to filing her nails, as though we weren't having one of the most important conversations of our lives. "Ms. Douglas told me she moved to Vermont for college and never wanted to come back, but when her dad got sick, she moved back to help her mom take care of him and never left again. But I'm going to get to Vermont and I'm not coming back."

The thought of Georgia leaving and never returning hurt my heart. I kept telling myself I'd be in Paris by then, but the truth was, it would be a miracle if I could earn enough money for that by the time Georgia would be going to Vermont. Next fall was just around the corner. How was I supposed to live here without her? I had to try and get to the American School of Paris for eighth grade. I had to!

"I need to live somewhere more open-minded." Georgia pointed her nail file toward me. "This whole place is stifling."

"That's just the humidity."

Georgia laughed.

I loved that I could make my sister laugh.

"I'm serious, Cleve. I'm leaving Sassafras next year and I'm never coming back."

I swallowed hard and pushed my blanket mountain away. "I'll bet they're open-minded in Paris, George. You could live there." In a quiet voice, I added, "With me."

"I'm sure they are, Cleve, but that's your big dream. Mine's Vermont."

"I know." *Why can't we have the same big dream?* "I'll miss you, that's all."

"And I'll miss you, Cleve, but I'll always love you. You'll always be my best sister."

"I'll always love you, George." I grabbed my blanket

145

again and hugged it extra hard. "But I'm your only sister."

It was so quiet in our room I could almost hear Georgia smile.

I turned and stared at the wall beside my bed, blinking, blinking. The weeks when Declan and I weren't hanging out and Dad being gone made me understand how bad it feels when someone you care about isn't around. My sister was leaving and never coming back. I wasn't going to be okay with that. My best friend was gay, which was A-OK, but it hurt that he wouldn't share this secret with me. Dad's brother, Larry, my uncle from California, was gay. He lived with his husband, Uncle Theo, and we had the best time when they visited, which was only once every couple of years. But since they moved to Belgium for Uncle Theo's job, we hadn't seen them at all. I decided I'd visit them all the time after I moved to Paris. Yet another reason to accomplish the items on my Paris Project list.

I rolled onto my stomach and thought about Declan. I guessed that cleared up the mystery of why Dec was always hanging out with Todd, why he looked at him the way he did at his locker. And why he wouldn't give up his friendship with Todd, even though he knew I wanted him to. What kind of friend was I that I didn't even realize? But didn't Dec feel he could trust me, Cleveland Rosebud Potts, his very best friend? He should have known I'd be his friend no matter what.

I turned toward my sister in the shimmery moonlight illuminating our room. "Hey, George?"

"Mhmm?"

"What do you think it will be like after Dad comes home?"

Georgia put her nail file down on the table between our beds and didn't say anything for a while.

"George?"

"I guess it will be the same as before he left, except . . ."

I held my blanket tight. "Except what?"

"Except we'll all worry he'll gamble again and fall into the same problems with stealing."

Georgia's voice sounded defeated.

I closed my eyes and remembered what happened the night Dad took my Eiffel Tower tin money.

Mom was waiting for him at the kitchen table. Her lips were pressed tight and she was tapping her foot.

I kept coming out of my room to check on her but pretended I was getting a drink or that I forgot a book on the table.

When Dad finally came home, I was in bed.

Georgia was in the shower, after her shift at work.

I heard the door open. Miss Genevieve's tags jingled, and I knew he was running over to greet Dad. Miss Genevieve was the only one in our house who wasn't angry with him.

I thought when Dad came in, Mom would yell, but I didn't hear her say anything.

"What?" Dad asked.

I had to strain to hear Mom. "I know what you did, John. Cleveland told me."

Dad was quiet.

"I can't think of anything worse. You stole from your kid."

"But I was going to . . . ," Dad started. "I'd planned to . . ."

"What?" Mom exploded. "You planned to win big this time? There is no 'big win,' John. Just you taking money from your daughter. Cleveland worked hard for that money."

Hearing Mom's words, knowing what Dad had done, pierced my heart. My dad had taken money from me. The Paris money I had worked so hard for. He was already going to jail for stealing from his boss, and still, he took money from me.

"And it's not okay!" Mom screamed, startling me.

Mom was right. She was sticking up for me, but I

148

wanted her to stop making Dad feel bad. Stop making things worse.

"I know. I know." I pictured Dad running a hand through his fine hair, hair that was just like mine. "But I—"

"No buts! You're already going to . . . You've got to knock this off! We can't afford it! You've got to . . . John? John . . . where are you going?"

The door slammed.

Miss Genevieve whined.

After a long silence, Mom let out one strangled sob that sounded like it would go on forever.

I shivered now, thinking about it, realizing Dad probably went right back to the dog park that night. He shouldn't have gone out and made Mom cry. I heard Georgia go to Mom after she came out of the bathroom. I heard her murmur soft words that I couldn't understand. I wished I'd done that—gone out and sat with Mom, put an arm around her shoulders, brought her a glass of water. Something. Or maybe run out after Dad and tried to stop him. I should have done something. But I was really upset with him and couldn't make myself do anything that night other than feel twelve kinds of sorry for myself.

With the moonlight streaming into our room, I lay

on my back and spoke to the ceiling, because it was easier than looking at Georgia while I talked about this.
"It's hard to trust a person after they do a thing like
that. Sometimes, George, when I go with Mom to visit
Dad, I'm so mad at him I don't even want to see him.
But at the same exact time, I feel sorry for him that he's
in there and want to reach through the screen and give
him a big hug and bring him home."

My sister didn't say anything. For a moment, I thought
she hadn't heard me or had fallen asleep. Then came a
whispery, "Oh, Cleve."

"It's okay," I lied. Why was I so confused about how
I felt? I should either hate him for what he'd done or
love him because he was my dad, but both of those
things were mixed together inside me.

"No. It wasn't okay." Georgia's voice was firm.
"Because you know what? A parent isn't supposed to do
that. They're supposed to take care of their kids, not
do things to hurt them. And what Dad did also made
everything harder for Mom. She has to work tons more
cleaning jobs now, and I still have to help her pay the
bills sometimes."

My heart sank like a stone. I hadn't realized Georgia
was helping Mom pay the bills. And it didn't occur to me
how much harder it would be without the money from

Dad's job and the extra cash he earned from repairing cars on weekends. I pictured the dark circles under Mom's eyes and how she almost always smelled faintly of bleach, like it was her favorite kind of perfume. I wished Mom smelled like gardenias, her favorite flower. "Yeah, that's terrible."

"Cleve?"

"Uh-huh?" I rolled onto my side toward my sister.

She turned over to face me and leaned on her elbow. "I'm real sorry Dad took your Paris money. I know how hard you worked for that. It stinks that he did that to you."

"Thanks, George. I'm sorry your college fund went to pay for his lawyer."

"*Our* college fund. I'm glad the money I earned from Weezie's was in a separate account at the bank and nobody needed it."

"Yeah. That's a real good thing." But I got a pang in my chest because the money I earned from all those dog walks had been in the Eiffel Tower tin under my bed and was gone forever. At least I was building it back up again.

"Hey, maybe I'll be able to earn enough money to put in a college fund for you, Cleve. You know, when you're ready for that."

My heart filled with love for my sister, because I knew she meant it. She'd work hard so I'd have money for school. She would do that for me, even if it meant she had to go without something herself. Like the way she'd paid for my ballet classes, even though I knew she needed that money for when she went to Vermont.

"Georgia?"

"Yeah?"

"Thanks for always having my back and looking out for me."

"Always."

Even though Dad was in jail, and I was pretty sure Declan had been keeping a big secret from me, I felt surprisingly good lying there in the magical glow of the moonlight with my big sister in the next bed and Mom and Miss Genevieve on the other side of the wall. It felt like everything would be okay.

"Good night, Cleve."

"Night, George."

Locker Talk

O N MONDAY MORNING DECLAN STRODE up to my locker with a hundred-watt smile. Even his pointy ears looked pink and happy.

Is Declan keeping anything else from me? "Hi, Dec."

"Hey, Scout." Declan pressed a folded piece of paper into my hand, his warm fingers touching mine. "For your Paris Project."

"My Paris Project?" Even though I hadn't had the heart to work on it these past weeks, Declan hadn't forgotten.

I couldn't keep from grinning as I unfolded the paper. It felt like unwrapping a birthday present. "Crepes!" I shouted, way too loud for our middle-school hallway.

Jenna Finch and her gang of girl followers happened to be walking by, of course. She shot me a look of disgust, but even Jenna's nasty face couldn't ruin my good mood. I waited until she and her evil minions were gone.

"That'll be perfect," I whispered to Declan.

Dec shook his head at those girls. "Small-minded," he muttered, which reminded me of my conversation with Georgia about her moving to Vermont. Then Declan focused on me, and his face brightened again. "I'm going to teach you how to make them. Savory ones and sweet ones." Declan leaned on the lockers. "I didn't forget, Scout."

I squeezed the paper to my heart. "You didn't forget, Dec."

"Hey, I just said that."

I shoved him playfully on the shoulder, and he pretended to fall all over the row of lockers.

Dec was back. He was going to teach me to make a French dish so I could accomplish the next item on my Paris Project list. He was still my friend.

"Hey, Maguire!" Robert Graham barreled toward us, his football jersey tight across his chest. I couldn't believe how big some of the eighth graders were. Graham got right in Declan's face. I noticed that he had a good few inches on Declan and the beginnings of a mustache. "Where's your *boy*friend?"

Declan's sweet smile melted away. He stepped toward Graham, shoving his chest out and standing tall. "Screw you!"

Ms. Baran, the music teacher, walked by us. "Language, boys," she said, as though it were Declan's fault.

As soon as Ms. Baran passed, I hissed, "Yeah, screw you, Graham!" I wanted to kick him hard in the shin but knew it would probably only hurt my foot, since my flimsy sneakers wouldn't provide much cushion, and I wasn't looking to get a broken toe.

"Aw," Graham said. "Isn't that cute, Maguire? You need your little seventh-grade friend defending you." He looked around, then gave Dec a vicious shove that knocked him backward into the lockers.

Graham eyed Declan, as if he were completely disgusted by being so close to him. I thought Graham was going to spit on him, but instead he turned and stormed off.

I hoped Declan hadn't landed on one of the locks. That would have hurt his back like a son of a bee sting.

"You okay?" I offered a hand, but Dec didn't take it. He righted himself, looking like he might cry, but then his nostrils flared and his cheeks flamed a deep shade of pink; I thought he'd turn and punch one of the lockers. I knew we were in school, but I wanted Declan to shout about how horrible Graham was. I wanted him to humiliate Graham for what he'd just done.

Anger boiled over inside me until my words exploded. "That guy's a jerk!"

Declan's lips pressed together. He got so close to my face I smelled banana on his breath. In a fierce whisper, so different from the tone he'd used with me only moments earlier, he said, "There are tons of jerks, Cleveland, but I don't need you defending me from them."

Dec was mad *at me*! "But—"

"I need . . ." Declan shook his head. "I need you to accept me. Who I am. Who I care about. That's it."

"I . . . I . . ."

Declan walked away.

I clutched the crepe recipe. *I do accept you, Dec. Of course I do. You never gave me a chance to tell you as much because you never told me about that part of yourself! And I'll do my best to accept Todd Baker, too. Of course I will. Even if his dad did something terrible to my dad. I'll do that for you, Declan Maguire, because you're my best friend.*

I squeezed the recipe in my fingers.

Aren't you?

Telling the Truth

AFTER WALKING MISS GENEVIEVE, Scarlett Bananas, Lucy, Trixie, and Colby (who was a sharp Shiba Inu that loved chasing squirrels), I cleaned up really good to wash away all the dog smells and headed over to Declan's, hoping he'd be the only one home.

"Scout!" Declan shouted when he opened the door.

He had a jagged scratch on his left cheek, like someone had played a sick game of connect the dots with a red pen and Declan's freckles.

"Come in," Dec said, as though nothing was wrong. "I'm starving but wanted to wait for you."

As soon as I stepped inside the trailer, I looked around to see if Todd was there.

"My dad's not here," Dec said. "He's teaching lessons at JAM over in Winter Beach."

"Oh," I said, as though I'd actually been looking for Mr. Maguire. "Dec, what happened to your face?" I reached up to touch the scratch.

He swatted my hand away. "It's nothing. Let's get started. Those crepes aren't going to cook themselves."

I was hungry and eager to get started, but that scratch on Declan's cheek bothered me. I remembered Graham shoving him this morning and guessed what *It's nothing* actually meant. Had this been happening for a while, but I was only now aware of it? I felt guilty for not noticing, not helping, not understanding sooner. If I'd known earlier, I could have helped protect Dec. I felt bad thinking people had been harassing him and I hadn't been there. I would want him to protect me if people were picking on me. He'd stuck up for me when Jenna started being mean at the beginning of sixth grade last year. But this morning Dec made it clear he didn't want my help, so I tried not to think about the scratch, who might have done it and why. "I'm so glad we're going to make crepes, Dec. Classic French dish."

"Indeed it is." Dec put on his toque—a real chef's hat that used to be his mom's; it had pictures of colorful cats all over it. He adjusted it so it rested on his head a little off center, the way, he told me, real chefs wore them.

I pictured Declan making fancy dishes with other chefs-in-training at Le Cordon Bleu in Paris. He'd probably be the only one with cats on his toque. I tugged on the sides of my beret. Both his toque and my beret felt perfectly French. Except for the wicked scratch on Dec's cheek, things were just right.

Declan scrubbed his hands at the kitchen sink and talked to me over his shoulder. "So, are we spending Halloween together, Scout?" He sounded defensive, like he was daring me to say no.

Inside, I was happy-dancing. "That would be great." I wanted to ask if it would be only the two of us, but I didn't want to hear the answer. Dad always told me not to ask a question if I wasn't ready to hear the answer. So I washed my hands and didn't say another word, while letting the thought of another Halloween with Declan ping-pong around the joy centers in my brain.

Declan put a canister of flour on the counter in front of us and took out a carton of eggs from the fridge. He also pulled out a slab of butter, a half gallon of milk, and some other ingredients. "Mind if Todd joins us?"

Declan asked, as though he were asking me if I could pass him the whisk.

Yes. Yes, I definitely mind. Halloween was always our thing, Declan Maguire, and you know that. "No," I said mouse-quiet.

"Okay. Good." Declan let out a breath. "I wanted to show him how cool that neighborhood is. Would you believe he's never gone out trick-or-treating? His family always has a big Halloween party at their house."

I thought of the times we'd gone to Todd's family's house for holiday parties and felt those familiar tendrils of anger slither around my belly.

"He's really excited about going with us."

You asked him before checking with me?

"That's great," I said with zero enthusiasm.

"Yeah, great," he said with plenty of enthusiasm.

I didn't want to think about Todd's family. "Can't imagine not trick-or-treating for your whole life," I said, to make conversation.

"Right?" Declan swiped at his scratch and grimaced.

"You okay?"

"Yeah. I'm fine."

He didn't sound fine. He sounded irritated.

Dec put a green plastic bowl in front of me. "Sift the flour, sugar, and salt into this."

When I dumped the flour into the sifter, a bunch got onto the counter. With ease, Declan added a bit more to make up for what I'd spilled. He always helped me and never made me feel bad that I wasn't very good in the kitchen. "Okay, now what?" I was glad my hands were busy so I could focus on something other than what we'd been talking about.

Declan put a bigger green plastic bowl in front of me. There wasn't much room on the counter at this point, and I was afraid I'd knock something to the floor, like I'd done in the past.

"You're okay," Dec said, as though he'd read my mind. "Now you need to beat the eggs and milk together." He helped me crack the eggs, but I measured and poured the milk. "You're supposed to use an electric mixer for this part, but we don't have one, so beat it really fast with the whisk."

That part was fun. I pretended the egg-and-milk mixture was Todd's head and beat it harder than I'd ever beaten anything in my life.

"Slow down, Scout." Declan laughed. "You're a whisking maniac over there."

This made me smile. "You should have an electric mixer, Dec. All the famous chefs online have them."

He shrugged. "I should have a lot of things, Scout."

I had a feeling he was talking about more than just kitchen equipment. Unfortunately, there was nothing I could do about what happened with his mom. Or the bullies at school. But maybe I could use some of my dog-walking money to buy him an electric mixer.

When all the ingredients were combined and Declan was heating the pan, he stopped and put his hand on my arm, the same way he'd touched Todd's arm the other day. "You sure you don't mind him joining us?"

My heart pounded. "Declan, do you, um . . ."

Declan cut a small chunk of butter and flipped it into the pan. It sizzled. "Do I what?"

I didn't want to mess anything up between us, but I had to know. My cheeks grew warm. "Do you like Todd?"

Declan turned down the heat under the pan. "Yeah. Sure. He's a good guy."

I noticed he didn't look at me when he answered. He swirled the butter around the pan with a spatula.

"I mean do you *like* him?"

Declan stopped fussing. He stood tall and turned toward me. "Yes."

It hurt that he hadn't told me sooner, hadn't shared this part of himself sooner, but here he was putting all his trust in me. I understood that the words I said next mattered. A lot. So I took a slow breath and gathered my thoughts. "That's really great, Declan."

Dec staggered backward, as though I'd pushed him. "Really, Scout? You . . . you're totally good with this? Even though it's Todd Baker?"

I tilted my head at my best friend, at his too-big ears and smattering of freckles bisected with a nasty scratch. I looked at his warm brown eyes and his lips that had smiled a million smiles at me. Declan Maguire had the biggest heart of anyone I knew besides my mom and sister and every dog on the planet. He always understood what I was going through and cared about it. He had big dreams of his own but acted like my dreams were *très importants.* "Declan, I'm a hundred percent good with this. Why wouldn't I be?" *As long as you still have a place for me to be your best friend.*

"Why wouldn't you be?" Declan shook his head, like he couldn't believe what he was hearing. "That's right, Scout. Of course. Why wouldn't you be?" He glowed.

I smiled.

Declan adjusted his toque and squared his shoulders. "Well, okay then. Let's make some crepes, *mon amie.*"

The French words for "my friend" sounded so good, as if he knew we would always be friends. "Yes, let's."

"Savory *and* sweet, Scout."

"Savory and sweet, Dec."

Without Georgia telling me, I knew I'd said the exact right thing to my friend when he most needed me to say it, and that made me feel wonderful.

Merveilleux!

Getting Closer

OM SWERVED INTO A PARKING spot at the video
visitation center.

"I wish I could bring Dad some of the
crepes Declan and I made on Monday."

"He would have loved that, Cleveland. Those crepes
were *délicieuses*. Did I say that right?"

"You did, Mom. Good job."

Mom pulled down her visor so she could use the
tiny mirror to put on lipstick. "Thanks. Guess that's
what happens when I pay attention to those French
language CDs you play." She patted my knee. "Don't
feel bad about not being able to give your dad the
crepes, Cleveland. You'll have plenty of opportunities

to make them for him when he gets home."

When he gets home.

I wiped the sweat off my upper lip. Seeing Dad on a video screen at a visitation center was one thing—we could pretend everything was okay for an hour—but him coming home forever would be something else entirely. There would be no pretending then. Would he stay away from the dog park? Would he be the dad he was before he loved to gamble? And how could we trust that he'd stay like that? How could I trust him at all?

Mom patted the top of the steering wheel. "Thank you for getting us here, Miss Lola Lemon." She treated cars the way I treated dogs—with lots of love and respect.

I tapped the dashboard. "You're a good old car."

"Shhh, Cleve. Don't tell Miss Lola Lemon she's old. She's sensitive about her age."

I shook my head at Mom.

"You ready?"

Maybe? "One sec." I fished inside the glove compartment and pulled out my list. It felt so good to check off the second item, to be moving forward with my big dream.

Thank you, Declan Maguire, chef and friend extraordinaire!

The Paris Project
By Cleveland Rosebud Potts

~~1. Take ballet lessons at Miss Delilah's School of Dance and Fine Pottery (to acquire some culture).~~
Ballet is not the answer . . . no matter what the question is!

√ 2. Learn to cook at least one French dish and eat at a French restaurant (to be prepared for the real thing). *Crepes—savory and sweet! Délicieuses!*

3. Take in paintings by the French impressionists, like Claude Monet's *Water-Lily Pond,* at an art museum so I can experience what good French art is (more culture!).

4. Continue learning to speak French (will come in handy when moving to France and needing to find important places, like *la salle de bains,* so I can go *oui oui*—ha-ha!—French bathroom humor).

5. Apply to the American School of Paris (must earn full scholarship to attend for eighth grade. You can do this, Cleveland!).

6. Move to France! *(Fini!)*
Good riddance, Sassafras, Florida!

I had no idea how I'd do the other half of the second item on my list: "eat at a French restaurant." They didn't even have one in Winter Beach, but at least I could cook a French meal now. And I definitely didn't know how I'd manage to do the third item on the list: go to a museum to see the French impressionists. But I was back to practicing along with the French language CDs from the library, which felt good because that was another step in the right direction.

I knew I could make this happen if I tried hard enough. It was amazing how much more positive I felt about achieving my big goal with Declan's support. It was so great knowing we were friends again.

Inside the visitation center, I glanced at the timer as Dad spent a full two minutes telling Mom how lovely she looked. I saw it made her happy by the way she sat taller but ducked her head. Then Dad seemed to notice I was there, sitting right next to Mom.

"Hey, Cleveland. So I'm dying to know. What will you and Declan dress as this year for Halloween?"

I realized Mom and Dad had no idea what had

happened between me and Declan. Dad probably assumed things were the same as when he went into jail. I guessed time sort of stopped for him, while things kept going in the world. It must be hard for people who are sent to prison for a much longer time.

I was glad Dad remembered to ask about my favorite holiday, but it made me sad, because it was his favorite holiday too. Dad always dressed up at Halloween, but he couldn't wear a silly costume this year and give out candy or go to any parties. He wouldn't have an opportunity to eat my Snickers bars and Reese's cups. I swallowed hard. "Well, Declan and I plan to go as French chefs. He's going to lend me the toque his dad gave him last year on his birthday. He'll carry a spatula. I'll carry a whisk. We'll both wear aprons." I shrugged.

"That sounds great, Cleve. Have a Snickers bar and a Reese's cup for me, if you get them."

"I will." Maybe when Dad came home, I'd buy him some of that candy.

I didn't tell Dad that Todd Baker planned to join us and was going to dress as a baseball player—the most boring costume ever. Dec said Todd was going to wear his actual baseball jersey and put some black gunk under his eyes. *Too bad he'll look like the odd one out, since Dec and I will be wearing matching costumes.*

"What have you been doing, Dad?"

"Hmm." Dad ran a hand through his hair, and I wondered if I'd asked the wrong question. "They have some car magazines in the lounge room that I've been looking through. And we watch *Jeopardy!* in the evenings like we did at home."

"That's awesome." I missed doing that with Dad.

"Tell you the truth, baby girl, I'd much rather watch it at home with you and yell our questions at the screen like we used to do."

Mom made a little hiccup sound.

"When I get home in February, we'll go out for ice cream and go swimming at the pool if it's not too cold, and then—"

"Time's up," the guard said.

I glanced at the timer and saw it flashing zero. "And I'm going to kick your butt in Monopoly!" Dad blew us a kiss and waved . . . then the screen went black. I was staring at an image of Mom squished next to me.

She squeezed my shoulders and leaned her head on mine. "This is hard," she whispered into my hair.

"Yup." I bit my bottom lip.

We held hands as we trudged outside, along with everyone else.

• • •

On the long, hot ride home in Miss Lola Lemon, I thought about how I could miss Dad so much and still feel stomach-clenching angry with him. It didn't make sense that both things could be happening inside me at the same time. I wished I could stop feeling all these things. "Hey, Mom?"

"Yeah, Cleve?" She kept her eyes on the road and tapped out a rhythm on the steering wheel to a song she must have heard only in her own head.

"Do you think you could help me with my application for the American School of Paris? There are a lot of forms. I printed them out at the library last week and started filling them out, but a couple need to be completed by a parent." I didn't add, *It's not like I can ask Dad to help.*

Mom glanced over at me. "You know I'd miss you like crazy cakes if you moved all the way to Paris, Cleveland Rosebud Potts."

I looked down at my lap. "I know."

"I'll help you with those forms, Cleve, if it's what you really want." She reached over and patted my knee.

I didn't want to leave Mom, Georgia, Dad, and Miss Genevieve. I didn't want to leave Declan. Of course I didn't. But I *had* to leave. I couldn't stand how people treated me at school anymore.

I recalled what happened in the lunchroom last Friday.

Sick of eating alone, I took a chance and sat at a table of girls I knew from PE class. As soon as I sat, one of the girls picked up her tray and turned to me. "I'm not sitting near you. We all know what your dad did to poor Todd Baker's dad. That makes you a lowlife, Cleveland. My mom wouldn't like me associating with people like that." She walked away. So did each of the other girls at the table.

I was alone. Again.

Alone and embarrassed, because no one wanted to sit with me, and apparently people were calling me names behind my back.

Glancing up, I saw Jenna watching me, a frown on her face. She'd probably seen the whole humiliating thing. Maybe this one time, Jenna would be kind. Maybe she'd understand how rotten I felt and smile to make me feel better. Maybe she'd remember when she wanted to hang out with me, when we used to have fun together. Perhaps she'd motion for me to come over to her table, let me sit with her and her friends, like before. Nope. Jenna smirked, her lip gloss all shiny and perfectly annoying, then went back to talking with the people at her table as if I didn't matter.

The car hit a bump and jarred me away from the painful memory. I stared out the open window, felt humid wind blow into my face, and watched the town of Sassafras whiz by, with its boarded-up businesses, tiny churches, and weathered billboards for guns and God.

I turned to Mom.

"It's what I want."

A Fallback

UT WHEN WE GOT HOME, Mom sat with Georgia and helped her with the application to the University of Vermont, so I walked Miss Genevieve and my weekend customers. We had brilliant conversations. I practiced asking where the bathroom was and where certain streets in Paris were located. Unfortunately, they barked at squirrels or ignored me entirely and went about their doggy business, so it was one-sided, but at least I got to rehearse my French vocabulary. I definitely planned to keep walking dogs after I moved to Paris. And they would all be wearing berets like mine.

Back inside our trailer, I scrubbed my hands at the kitchen sink and realized Mom and Georgia were having a heated discussion.

"Please, Georgia," Mom said, reaching a hand across the table.

Georgia held on to her laptop like a shield. "No."

Mom turned to me. "Cleveland, talk some sense into your sister."

I put my hands up. I had no idea what they were arguing about, so I filled up Miss Genevieve's water bowl and listened in.

"Georgia, you're so smart, but sometimes smart kids don't get to go where they want for college. Apply to a couple other schools in case you don't get into the University of Vermont. You know, as a fallback."

Georgia slammed her laptop closed. "Thanks for the confidence, Mom. But I'm getting in. I don't need a fallback school. I've worked too hard to need one."

Mom pulled her hand back and put it in her lap. "Georgia," Mom said quietly. "A couple other schools won't hurt. Apply. Just in case."

I leaned against the kitchen counter.

Georgia let out a big breath. "Mom, it costs money to apply to each school. It's expensive!"

"I'll pay for it."

"Mom." Georgia tilted her head. "You barely have enough money to—"

"I know. I know." Mom looked down; I remembered when Georgia had told me she sometimes helped Mom pay our bills. "Okay," Mom said. "I guess there's always community college as a fallback."

Georgia slapped a palm on the table, which startled Miss Genevieve. "I don't need a fallback! I'm definitely not going to community college in stupid Sassafras."

"Stupid Sassafras." I snickered.

Mom gave me a pointed stare, then turned back to Georgia. "That's why you should apply to a couple other places."

"Maybe I can help," I said. "I have over four hundred dollars in my Paris Project fund. I can give you some money toward the application fees, George." I sat on the floor and scratched behind Miss Genevieve's ears, the way he liked it, remembering how Georgia pulled out those twenty-dollar bills from her I ♥ VERMONT wallet to pay for my dance class. "I'd be happy to do it."

"Thanks, Cleve. But I'm not applying anywhere else. It's a waste of money and time."

Mom tapped the table with her fingernail. "Georgia, it's that—"

"Let it go, Mom! I applied to Vermont. You should congratulate me. A lot of kids in my class aren't applying to any colleges."

Mom bit her bottom lip. "You work hard and do well, George. You deserve to go to Vermont. I just don't . . ."

Mom didn't finish her sentence.

Georgia picked up her computer, walked into our bedroom, and shut the door.

I moved into her space at the table, across from Mom. "So, do you have time now to help me with the application forms for the American School of Paris?"

"Not now, Cleveland!"

Mom stood and shook out her shoulders. She looked upset. "I'm sorry, sweetheart. I'm a little stressed right now. It's not a good time." She went into her room and closed the door.

With two closed bedroom doors ahead of me, I curled up next to Miss Genevieve on the floor, patting the soft white fur over his rib cage, which rose and fell with each slow doggy breath. "Some of the pages have to be filled out by a parent," I whispered. "If Mom doesn't help, I'll be stuck here in Sassafras when Georgia leaves for Vermont." Saying it out loud hurt my heart.

I kissed Miss Genevieve on his head and went to our bedroom to be with my sister, because I knew even if she was upset, Georgia would never be mean to me. She'd be glad for my company, she'd want me to sit near her, unlike certain awful girls at Sassafras Middle School.

When it came to sisters, I'd hit the lottery.

Are You Sure?

"CLEVELAND, IF I NEVER SEE another form to fill out for school or financial aid, I will be a happy woman."

"I know it's a lot, Mom." I watched over her shoulder as she filled out the medical form for the American School of Paris. I felt tingly all over realizing we were moving closer to my goal, completing actual paperwork instead of only talking about it. It had taken Mom two weeks since the blowup with Georgia to find time to help me with this. "I really appreciate it."

Mom reached up and touched my cheek. "I know you do, baby."

"Want me to make you a snack?"

"Popcorn would be great."

Miss Genevieve's ears perked up as the bag circled inside the microwave. He knew I'd give him a couple of pieces after it cooled off.

"Cleveland?" Mom's voice was laced with concern. "Have you looked at the cost of applying? I mean, it's listed in euros, but holy hippos, that's a ton of money."

My stomach tightened. "I know it's expensive, Mom, but I've been saving a lot of money from my dog walks. I'm up to six hundred ten dollars already, and next week I'll have seven hundred."

Mom got up and massaged her temples as she looked into the microwave. "That is a lot of money."

"Right?" I puffed out my chest, feeling proud.

The kernels had started to pop, and buttery deliciousness filled the air.

Mom leaned on the counter and brushed off some crumbs. "Cleve, I don't want you to get your hopes up because, honey, I don't think there are enough dogs in the world to walk to earn the kind of money it would take to go to this school. And I didn't see anything on their site about scholarships. Also, you'd have to find housing somewhere. That's probably expensive too."

I bit my bottom lip. "It's a lot of money because it's such a great school. And I couldn't find scholarships either." I deflated a little. The scholarships were an important part of my plan. The school cost almost forty thousand a year in American dollars, plus a bunch of other fees, and that didn't even include the travel to get over there and someplace to live. I didn't know how I'd get the money, but I knew I had to try. Even if I couldn't get there for eighth grade next year, maybe I could start high school in Paris. Maybe we'd win the lottery or I'd get another job. I felt a tightening in my chest. *Is that what Dad thought when he went to the dog park all those times, that he'd win lots of money for us?* Maybe I wouldn't earn enough to get to Paris, but I couldn't give up and stay here in Sassafras, not with the way the kids at school thought about me, and the way the neighbors looked at me. No way could I stay! *Pas question!*

"Cleve, the capital assessment fee alone is more than ten thousand dollars." Mom sucked in a sharp breath. "Do you know how many houses I'd have to clean to earn that much money?"

I nodded, even though I had no idea. "A lot."

"Yes, a *lot!*"

I took out the popcorn and poured it into two bowls, even though my appetite had evaporated during our conversation.

"Sweetheart, are you a hundred percent sure you

want to move forward with your plans for Paris?"

I felt tears well up because I had tried not to think about how expensive the school was. I closed my eyelids against the tears and nodded. "I'm sure, Mom."

She put an arm around my shoulders. "Okay then. Let's get back to those forms."

I suddenly got hungry. "Okay."

While Mom finished filling out the medical questionnaire, I worked on the candidate questionnaire and autobiography.

Each of us gave Miss Genevieve a few pieces of popcorn.

I stopped worrying about the cost and allowed wisps of hope to float back inside myself. "Thanks, Mom."

"You know, Cleveland," Mom said. "That school would be lucky to have you."

My Formerly Favorite Holiday

DECLAN AND I WERE DECKED out in aprons and toques and had our kitchen implements ready when there was a pounding on the Maguires' trailer door.

My stomach dropped. I'd hoped Todd would come down with a sudden illness that would make it impossible for him to join us for trick-or-treating. Nothing too dreadful, just a twenty-four-hour virus or a horrible case of flatulence. This would be our last year. Next year Dec would be going into high school, and high schoolers didn't go trick-or-treating. I didn't want to share my last Halloween with Todd Baker. I'd wished Mr. Baker would insist Todd stay home for their annual family party, but apparently that hadn't happened either, because there he was, pounding on the Maguires' door like he was the police or something; my heart hammered.

But the way Declan's eyes lit up at the sound reminded me that he wanted Todd to join us, to be part of our annual tradition.

Dec flung open the door. "Hey!"

I stood back, leaning on the kitchen counter.

Todd came in wearing his baseball jersey, with black makeup under his eyes and a dopey grin. He gave Declan a tight hug and waved to me behind Dec's back.

I wiggled a couple of fingers at him and looked down. My dad was in jail right now and *not* dressed up for Halloween because of Todd Baker's dad. Anger bubbled inside me. I wished I were wearing my beret, because it made me feel closer to Dad. How had I not realized how good I had things last year when Declan and I went trick-or-treating by ourselves, and Dad was dressed as a mechanic with a unicorn horn, giving out candy with Mom, who was dressed as Rosie the Riveter, outside our trailer? I sighed. Tonight Mom was home by herself. She'd said she didn't feel like giving out candy this year.

"How's it going, Cleveland?" Todd asked.

I shrugged. *You are ruining my last Halloween with Declan.*

"Great costume!" Declan hit Todd in the chest with the back of his hand.

Todd tipped his baseball cap at him.

At least the cap covered his weird hair bump.

Mr. Maguire came out from his bedroom. "You kids ready for some serious trick-or-treating?" He rubbed his palms together. "Good candy, here we come!"

"Hey, *you're* not getting candy," Dec said.

Mr. Maguire grabbed his keys. "Oh, didn't I tell you there's a fee of ten percent of the candy you get for driving you dingbats all the way out to Winter Beach?"

"Boo!" Dec yelled.

"You can have fifteen percent of my candy," Todd said.

"Suck-up." Dec shoved him.

Todd laughed and shoved him back.

Why do they keep touching each other?

I was glad when we grabbed our pillowcases and piled into Mr. Maguire's car. The trailer felt too small for all of us. At least it did after Todd walked into it.

Dec sat in the backseat next to Todd. I didn't think there was enough room back there for me, so I sat in the front passenger seat, feeling left out.

Mr. Maguire put on some fiddle music. The boys whispered and laughed behind me. To cheer myself up,

I thought about the kinds of candy we might get at the big houses we visited, like full-size Hershey bars, and maybe some of them would give out money if they ran out of candy early. I promised myself I'd save some of Dad's favorite candy, even if it was stale by the time he got home in February. It seemed so far away. The candy would definitely be stale by then . . . if ants didn't get to it first. I slumped in my seat.

I peeked in the back. Declan and Todd were holding hands.

I stared straight ahead the rest of the ride and concentrated on the fiddle music. I didn't need to be reminded that Todd was replacing me as Declan's most important friend.

Mr. Maguire waited for us in the car with his fiddle music playing and a thick Stephen King novel, which he said was perfect for a good scare on Halloween.

We walked around the neighborhood of fancy houses with big front yards and porches. I walked ahead of Dec and Todd because there wasn't enough room on the sidewalk for three of us.

Someone poked me in the back. I turned and smiled because I thought it was Declan trying to get my attention, but it wasn't. It was Todd.

Todd Baker poked me in the back.

My expression turned from happy to annoyed confusion.

"Hey, Cleveland," Todd said. "Did you know the Eiffel Tower was the world's tallest building until 1930?"

At first I thought Todd was mentioning Paris to make me feel bad because I'd been so upset lately about not knowing how I was going to afford going to school over there. But then I realized Declan must've shared my Paris plan with Todd, and he cared enough to learn something about the City of Lights.

"Yeah, I did," I said. "But that's a really cool fact." If Todd could do that for me, I could try to be nice to him. For one lousy night. For Declan.

Todd nodded. "It seems like a really great place to want to live, Cleveland."

I opened my mouth. Then closed it. Then opened it again, but nothing came out.

Declan tilted his head at me, as if to say, *See, I told you he was cool.*

It would take more than one interesting fact about Paris to change my mind about Todd Baker. I stormed up the long walkway to the first house, squeezing my whisk a little too tightly, trying to hang on to my anger. Todd was not cool. He was not thoughtful. He was the son of the guy who'd put my dad in jail. He was a traitor to me and my family. I had to remember that.

Because on top of everything else, he was now ruining Halloween for me too.

"So how'd you do?" Mr. Maguire asked when we approached the car with full pillowcases and tired feet.

"Très bien!" I said at the same time Todd said, *"Merveilleux!"* which meant "wonderful" in French.

Dec and I both looked at him.

He shrugged. "I know a few French words. No big deal."

"Yes, big deal," Dec said.

I shook my head. "Why?"

"Hmm?" Todd asked.

"Why did you learn some French words?"

Todd tugged on the rim of his baseball cap. "Because Dec told me you love everything French."

Dec looked at me.

"I do." But that didn't mean Todd Baker had to go and learn some basic French. But he did.

"Get in, kids," Mr. Maguire said. "I'm ready to go home and raid your candy stash. Don't forget you owe me twenty percent of everything."

"You said ten percent," Dec reminded him.

"No one likes a know-it-all, kid."

We piled into the car, laughing.

It didn't feel so bad being in the front seat on the way home because Declan and Todd included me in their conversation about the world's best restaurants. I didn't have much to add, but the talk was making me hungry.

Back at Declan's trailer, we dumped out our bags of candy on the kitchen table.

"Yes!" I snatched out two Reese's Peanut Butter Cups and set them aside for Dad.

Declan and Todd were staring at me.

"My dad loves those," I said, immediately wishing I could take back the words. I didn't want to talk about my dad, especially in front of Todd.

Before I knew it, Todd had handed me the two Reese's Peanut Butter Cups from his pile.

It felt like an apology, those candies. I didn't want to accept them, but Dad once told me it was hard for people to apologize, and the right thing to do was to take someone's apology when they offered it. He'd been referring to the one time Georgia and I got in a fight over using the bathroom: she apologized to me but I stayed angry. Dad wasn't having it.

I took Todd's candy and added it to my "Dad" pile. "Thank you."

Todd nodded.

Declan nodded too.

In that moment, over a couple of Reese's Peanut Butter Cups, something shifted between me and Todd Baker.

And it felt good.

Maybe Halloween wasn't a complete waste after all.

Declan and Todd walked me home, because sometimes at night certain people drank beer outside their trailers and were kind of loud. It was better not to walk by myself.

Back home, Mom was already in her room.

I knocked on her door.

"Come in."

She had the blanket pulled up to her neck and was looking through a photo album. She moved over and patted the space beside her.

The photos were of all the crazy costumes Dad and she had worn on Halloweens past.

Mom patted my hand. "I'm really missing him tonight."

I squeezed her hand. "Me too. I saved his favorite candy for when he gets home."

Someone knocked on the door.

"Come in," Mom and I called at the same time.

Georgia stood in the doorway in her pajamas and fuzzy purple socks. "Move over, Cleveland."

The three of us squished into the bed and looked through the photo album together.

"This is so tough sometimes," Georgia said.

"Really tough," I agreed, wishing I'd taken a minute to grab my beret, because it would help make me feel better.

"At least we're together," Mom said, leaning into me. "That helps."

I leaned into Georgia. She leaned back.

Miss Genevieve let out a fierce snore from the foot of the bed, and we all laughed.

Something Changed

HAT MONDAY IN SCHOOL, EVERYONE had Halloween candy in addition to their lunches.

I wished someone else were at my table, because it would be fun to see what candy they had and trade with them. All I could do was watch the other kids doing this at their tables. Lunch dragged on forever. I nibbled on the peanut butter and jelly sandwich Georgia had made me and wished I had a book with me, like *Madeline*, but that would give people like Jenna Finch another reason to be mean to me. But I still wished I had one, especially the story where they adopted the hero dog, Miss Genevieve. That was my favorite.

At least I had my beret.

The rest of the school day was quiet, but at the end something happened.

I was at my locker when Jenna came over to her locker. She was ignoring me as usual.

Then Todd Baker approached.

At first my stomach clenched at the sight of him, but he walked toward me with a big grin on his face.

"Scout!" he shouted.

Todd Baker had called me Scout. It made my heart thump the same way it did when Declan said it.

He leaned over and gave me a big hug . . . right in front of Jenna and her perfect hair.

His hug completely surprised me, but it made me feel good, too. Wanted. Cared about. And the best part was how big Jenna's eyes grew. She looked more surprised than I felt.

Before Todd walked away, he said, "Hey, come over to Declan's later. He's trying out a new recipe."

"Oh . . . okay."

Then Todd high-fived me and walked away.

He'd used my special name, hugged me, invited me to Declan's, and high-fived me. All those things had happened right in front of Jenna Finch.

I smiled on the walk home and realized something amazing. When Todd Baker came into Declan's life, I'd thought I was losing my best friend. I wasn't. I was gaining a new one.

Todd wasn't just Declan's boyfriend.

He was also my friend.

Mon ami.

Thankful, But . . .

THANKSGIVING WAS WEIRD.

Dad used to make the meal, and Mom would get a salad together. Georgia and I usually relaxed all day and didn't do anything, which was glorious.

Not this year.

Since Mom had the day off from cleaning people's houses, she took a nap in the afternoon. Georgia and I made dinner for the three of us—noodles with Newman's Own tomato-and-basil pasta sauce, green beans, and a sweet potato pie that Declan gave me the recipe *and* the sweet potatoes for.

I peeled the potatoes into a bowl with great

vengeance. "I don't think I'm going to get to Paris."

Georgia knocked her hip into mine. "Don't say that, Cleve. Just keep doing the things on your list. It'll happen . . . someday."

I stopped peeling. "That's exactly it, George. I'm stuck. How am I going to eat at a French restaurant or go to a museum and see works from famous French impressionists? Not to mention get the money I need to go. It's soooooo expensive."

Georgia leaned on the counter. "Hmm. I'm not sure. But we'll figure it out."

It made me feel good that my sister said "*we'll* figure it out."

"Hey, I got my application, fee, and essay in to the University of Vermont way ahead of the deadline, so that's awesome."

"That is awesome!" I was excited for my sister, even though I wasn't excited for myself because that meant next year I'd be here without her.

"Thanks, Cleve. I probably won't hear until late February, but at least I did my part. It's all I can do for now. Except wait."

I sliced the peeled sweet potatoes and dropped them into a pot of water, then set it to boil. "I'm going to miss you."

"Huh?"

"When you go to Vermont. I thought I'd be off to Paris when you went to the university, but now . . ."

Georgia wrapped her arms around me. She accidentally banged my head and knocked my beret off. My naked head reminded me of that awful day at dance school with Jenna Finch, who was probably having a perfect Thanksgiving dinner with her whole family in their fancy house.

"Sorry," Georgia said.

"It's okay." I put my beret back on.

"You've still got plenty of time to get to Paris, Cleveland."

"Yeah, but nothing is going like it's supposed to. Maybe someday I'll be Mom's age, looking at travel magazines and still not going anywhere."

My sister didn't say anything after that, and we cooked the rest of the meal with the only noise coming from Miss Genevieve's quiet snoring.

That is, until Georgia put on some holiday music. That lifted my mood a little.

When everything was ready, Georgia set the table and took the pie out of the oven. "Go tell Mom dinner's ready."

I shuffled to her door and knocked softly in case she was still napping.

"Come in!"

Mom was sitting up in her bed, thumbing through a magazine. "Dinner ready?" She put the magazine on her nightstand.

I nodded, but a tidal wave of emotion spewed out. Mom. The travel magazine. Dad's empty side of the bed. It was too much to take today. My breath caught and my shoulders hitched. Before I knew it, tears streamed down my cheeks like someone had opened a spigot.

"Oh, Cleve. Come here."

I climbed in and pulled the blanket up to my chin.

Mom slid an arm around my shoulders. "Now, you tell me what's the matter."

"I . . . I . . ." I couldn't stop crying long enough to tell her, and I wasn't even sure exactly what it was. Everything was all jumbled up inside.

Mom whispered into my beret, "We're going to get through this, sweetheart."

The truth of it brought a fresh round of tears. I nodded hard, then choked out three words: "I . . . hate . . . this." I grabbed a tissue off Mom's night table and wiped my eyes and nose.

Mom pulled me closer. "I hate it too, Cleveland."

"Me too." Georgia leaned on the doorframe. "Can I join the party?"

Mom made room for Georgia on the other side of her. It was just like Halloween. Miss Genevieve hopped onto the end of the bed where he used to curl near Dad's feet. Then he snorfled himself into a cozy heap.

"Only a little over two months till he comes home," Mom said.

I nodded.

"And there's something else." Mom pushed my hair out of my eyes. "When he comes out, he has to go to Gamblers Anonymous meetings."

"He does?" Georgia asked.

Mom nodded. "That should help Dad stay on track. We'll be okay, girls. Just have to hang on a little longer."

I sniffed.

We all squished closer to each other.

It made me feel better. All of us together; four peas in a pod. And hopefully, Dad having to go to a program would help him not gamble. Maybe we wouldn't have to worry so much. I had saved a lot of money from all my dog walks—I was at almost a thousand dollars—and I didn't want anything to happen to it.

We ended up eating Thanksgiving dinner in Mom's bed.

It wasn't such a terrible holiday after all.

Another Holiday That Wasn't Entirely Terrible: Part 2

WE GOT THROUGH CHRISTMAS TOGETHER too.

Mom put extra money in Dad's account at jail so he could buy himself some holiday treats. When we visited, he said they were planning a little party there. Mom and I wore Santa hats for our visit. (I wore mine over my beret.) The sheriff at the visitation center let us wear them, and I'm glad because they made Dad laugh out loud.

On Christmas, Aunt Allison came over with my cousin, Ellen, who just turned six. I wished they didn't live so far away so we could see them more often.

Ellen spent the whole time twirling and telling us how much she wanted to be a ballerina. I gave my cousin the bag with all my ballet clothes, and I've never seen a person so excited. She put the clothes on—which were way too big on her, especially the ballet slippers—and danced the entire rest of the time. I almost told her to be careful about getting runs in the tights, but I didn't. I let her enjoy herself, like a person should when they're dancing.

A while later Declan and his dad came over.

The trailer was cramped with all of us inside, but I didn't mind. It felt cozy and filled with joy. Everyone seemed genuinely happy for the first time in months.

Declan had made two strawberry rhubarb pies, which were of course delicious. I had seconds, and Ellen had thirds, but it was wasted on her because she ended up barfing it all up in our bathroom.

"It's from all that twirling," Aunt Allison said.

"And pie!" Ellen said helpfully.

We laughed.

Then Mr. Maguire played his fiddle late into the night.

I sat next to Declan on the kitchen bench seat. It felt good leaning against him, listening to the music, being surrounded by family and friends.

Mom and Georgia bought me a cute outfit with black leggings and a red-and-white-striped top they said would be perfect to wear on my first day in Paris.

"It'll match your beret," Mom said.

"You'll look like a mime," Georgia added, so I pretended to be stuck behind a glass wall, knocking on the air between us.

This made Mom smile.

Georgia shook her head at me.

I didn't tell them I thought I'd never get a chance to wear it because I was absolutely stuck on how I'd accomplish the other items on my Paris Project list and also the money thing. Instead I gave them each a bone-crunching hug.

Declan gave me a book about visiting Paris. It had maps and lots of photos. I gave Declan a French cookbook I'd been saving from the library book sale last year.

"I'll start in on these recipes," Dec said, "as soon as I finish the ones in my mom's cookbook."

I nodded quietly, realizing Dec was probably thinking about his mom the way I was thinking about my dad today. No matter how much fun we were having, there was always that part of us missing the people who weren't here. Except next Christmas my dad would be with us. Declan's mom never would.

I couldn't understand how anyone would walk away from them. They were two of the best people I knew. Then she left forever. I don't know how I would be feeling if I knew I'd never be able to see Dad again.

Life could be so hard sometimes.

That was why it was smart to focus on the good moments when you could.

I decided to focus on the positive things during our Christmas celebration.

There was a lot to be happy about.

Plus, we were getting closer to Dad's release date.

A little over one month to go!

Home

O N THE DAY OF DAD'S release, Mom went to the jail by herself to get him. She took the day off from work. Georgia and I stayed home from school.

Fortunately, Miss Lola Lemon decided to behave that day and started with no problem.

That morning I counted how much money was in my Eiffel Tower tin. I hadn't checked in a while and was delighted that the amount totaled $1,870.

I put my money back inside and shoved it under my bed, thinking I should find a better hiding place now that Dad was coming home. Even though it wouldn't get me to Paris yet, it was a lot of money and I didn't want to lose it again. Of course, thinking that made me feel guilty. I should be able to let it go and trust Dad. *Right?*

I knew I should give him the benefit of the doubt, especially since he'd be going to Gamblers Anonymous meetings. Mom had explained that wouldn't keep Dad from wanting to gamble, but it would help him if he decided to help himself. Only Dad could make the decision not to gamble each day, Mom said. All we could do was hope he stayed away from the dog park.

Georgia and I kept getting in each other's way as we cleaned the trailer, cooked lunch, and baked two trays of oatmeal raisin cookies made with bananas—Dad's favorite.

At one point I accidentally stepped on Miss Genevieve's paw, and he yelped. "Sorry, boy." I patted his soft head until he settled back down.

Then I looked at my sister. "You nervous?"

"Yes!"

We laughed, but it didn't ease the tension.

As the delicious smell from the cookies baking wafted through the trailer, I heard Miss Lola Lemon pull into the gravel driveway.

"They're home," Georgia whispered.

I gulped.

Miss Genevieve was going nuts at the door, running

in circles and barking. Very un-Miss-Genevieve-like. Napping was Miss Genevieve's preferred state of being.

Georgia and I stood behind Miss Genevieve at the door.

My sister chewed on a fingernail. "You ready for this, Cleve?"

I wasn't but nodded anyway.

Georgia opened the door.

There in front of the steps was Dad . . . dancing with Mom. He twirled her in circles again and again, and when Mom finally lost her balance and wobbled, they cracked up. Mom looked ridiculously happy. Happier than she'd looked during the past seven months.

Dad looked happy too, but he had stubble on his face and was even thinner, if that was possible. His clothes were hanging on him. I was glad we'd baked cookies and made lunch for him.

Miss Genevieve rocketed outside. He jumped on Dad, his front paws up, like he was hugging him. Miss Genevieve yipped and whined so hard it sounded like he was crying.

Dad pet him hard. "Oh, Roscoe. I missed you so much, buddy."

Miss Genevieve turned in circles, then started all

over again with the jumping and whining. It seemed like it would go on forever.

Other people were outside their trailers, some with their arms crossed—still judging us—while others had smiles on their faces over our happy reunion. Ms. Welch was out there, clutching her flowered bathrobe. Didn't that woman ever wear regular clothes when she came out to spy on neighbors?

It didn't matter.

None of it.

Let them stare.

My family was together again!

Georgia and I ran down the steps and into Dad's arms. Dad wrapped us fiercely in his tight grip, like he'd never let us go.

My cheeks were wet. I couldn't help it.

When I looked up, I saw Dad was crying too. Mom joined us, and Dad tried to wrap us all in his arms.

I couldn't have imagined how good it would feel to have Dad home.

Miss Genevieve jumped and barked, wanting to be part of the family reunion.

"Oh my God, I missed you all so much." Dad sobbed openly.

"We're so glad you're home, John."

"Yeah, Dad," Georgia said. "We made you lunch."

"And cookies!" I shouted.

Everyone laughed and cried because . . .

Dad.

Was.

Finally.

Home!

Hope?

I N LESS THAN A WEEK, my parents were arguing in the kitchen.

Georgia was at work, but I was home in our bedroom, reading. Our trailer was so small that I could hear every word. I pulled the blanket up to my chin, wishing Miss Genevieve were in bed with me, but I knew he was out with my parents because he kept whining. Miss Genevieve didn't like when anyone in the house argued.

"I can't stand seeing you work this much, Glory. It's not good for you."

I pictured Mom's hand on her hip. "What do you want me to do, John? We need the money."

"I know we need the money, but . . ." I imagined Dad running his hand through his thin hair.

I chewed on my thumbnail. Why couldn't they be happy like they were the day Dad came home?

"We're still paying off your lawyer's bill. I had to take as many cleaning jobs as I could, John."

"I'm sorry, Glory. How many times can I tell you that? I'll build it all back. It's just that . . ."

Silence.

Then Dad spoke so softly I had to strain to hear. "I can't get a job."

There was something in Dad's words—a feeling. It was the same feeling I had when those stupid ballet girls laughed at me, when the neighbors looked at us with judgment in their eyes, when women whispered about us in the market, when the girls from my gym class got up from the lunch table—away from me. Shame.

"You'll get a job. You're a great salesman and a talented mechanic. If not, maybe you could work in a restaurant or—"

"You're not listening to me, Glory!"

Miss Genevieve barked.

"It's okay, Roscoe." I figured Dad was petting Miss Genevieve, to keep him calm. "No one wants to hire someone who's been in jail, Glory. That's the problem. I know I can do the work. I've put in dozens of applications all over town and in Winter Beach, too, but the minute I fill in that part about being convicted of a crime . . ."

"John, I'm sure someone will . . ."

Mom didn't finish.

"I need to find a way to make money right now." Dad pounded on something—maybe the kitchen counter. "We need money now. You need to work less now. We need to build the college fund back up now."

"It'll be okay," Mom said in a soothing voice. "I don't mind taking on the extra cleaning jobs."

Nobody spoke for a while, then Mom's voice: "To tell the truth, John, I worried this would happen when you got out. I worried people wouldn't give you a chance. At least the court didn't take away your driver's license. That was something they could have done too. I'm glad you still have that. We'll figure it out, babe. It'll be okay."

"No! It won't be okay. Nothing will be okay anymore. Don't you get it?"

Miss Genevieve barked and barked.

"I'm going out," Dad said hurriedly.

"John!"

Our trailer door opened and slammed shut.

I shuddered and clutched my blanket under my chin. Why did everything have to be so hard?

I heard Mom go into the bathroom and run the water. Then she closed the door of their bedroom. Soft sobs erupted.

I wanted to run to her, but I couldn't move from the spot in my bed. I waited till the sounds stopped. Then I tiptoed to her bedroom and knocked quietly. No answer. I knocked harder.

"Come in."

Mom was sitting up in bed with a box of tissues cradled in her arms. Her eyes were pink and puffy.

"I'm sure I look all a mess." She waved a hand in front of her face.

Her hair stuck out in a million different directions. "You look great." I climbed into bed next to her.

"Your dad went out."

"Yeah, I heard."

"I guess you did. Not much privacy in our house, is there? Sorry about that."

I wasn't sure if Mom was sorry that I heard them yelling or sorry we lived in a tiny house. Either way, she didn't have anything to apologize for. I picked at the fibers at the edge of her blanket. "Mom, do you think . . ."

She put an arm around my shoulders and sniffed. "What, Cleve?"

Words choked out: "Do you . . . think he's . . . going to the dog park?"

Mom pulled me closer to her. She leaned her head against mine. "Well, baby girl, we can't know that. Can we?"

"But . . . I don't want him to go there anymore. I wish that place closed down."

"I know, sweetheart." Mom kissed my head. "Like I said, your dad needs to figure this out. We can't keep him from gambling. Only he can do that."

My shoulders drooped, because I didn't know if he *could* do that. A hopeless feeling crept inside me and nestled deep.

"All we can do is wait," Mom said. "And hope."

Now there was a word I could hang on to.

Hope. *L'espoir.*

But in addition to hoping, there was one other thing I could do.

Just to be safe.

Getting Left . . . Twice

I KISSED MOM ON HER DAMP cheek, went to my room, and pulled my Eiffel Tower tin from under the bed.

The walk to Declan's didn't take long, especially with my sure and determined strides. There was no way I was losing my money a second time. I loved all the dogs, but it was hard work to walk them in the heat every day and pick up after them.

I knocked on the trailer door, hoping Declan was there by himself.

"Scout!" Dec wore jean shorts and a ripped T-shirt and no shoes. "You look like you need a spritzer. Come on in."

I let out the breath I'd been holding and loosened

my grip on the Eiffel Tower tin. "Extra lime, please."

After Declan had prepared our drinks, and I'd had a few fizzy swallows, I told him all about the argument my parents had had and how Dad had taken off for what was probably the dog park.

"I hope that's not it, Scout."

"Me too." I took another shaky sip. "But could you hang on to my Paris money just in case?"

"Of course." Dec smiled. "Hey, Scout, your dad probably just went for a walk or something."

I shrugged. "This was how it was when he'd go gamble. He and Mom would fight, and then he'd storm out and not come home till a million hours later. It was awful, and I don't want to go back to how it was back then."

Declan looked down. "Hey, at least you have your dad."

He was right. "Yeah, we were all so glad when he finally came home, but now—"

"No." Dec pulled at a thread at the bottom of his T-shirt. "At least you *have* your dad."

Then I understood what he meant. Declan wasn't talking about my dad. He was talking about his mom.

"Sorry, Dec. Yes. I'm lucky to have him at all. You're right."

He tapped on the table with one finger. "You know the worst thing, Scout?"

He didn't seem like he was quite there with me anymore, like he was lost in a memory. Even though I'd never met her, Declan's mom—what happened to her—was the sad note that ran through everything, like Declan's cooking, his dad's music. "What's that, Dec?" I asked real quiet.

"I got left not once, but twice." Dec laughed, but it wasn't a funny laugh.

I bit my bottom lip and let a wobbly breath escape.

He pushed his drink away. "When Mom left with the other cook at that restaurant, I thought it was the worst thing ever. I wondered how she could abandon Dad and me like that. I hated her. . . . We had to move here since Mom made most of our money, and Dad was only giving a few music lessons and hardly ever got live gigs back then. We ate cheap spaghetti with no sauce and whatever canned vegetable was on sale that week. It was quite a change from the good stuff Mom used to cook for us."

I reached across the table and gave Dec's hand a quick squeeze, so he'd know he could tell me the rest.

"It hurt getting left like that. For a long time I thought it was my fault and I really did hate my mom. But then . . ."

I swallowed hard. "You don't have to say it, Dec. You don't."

216

"Yeah." He nodded. "I do. When she was riding on the motorcycle with that guy. That jerk."

"Jerk," I said softly.

"When she was riding on the motorcycle with him instead of being home with Dad and me . . ."

I touched the back of his hand.

He shook my fingers off. "When it was raining . . . and they were riding together on that motorcycle and . . . they skidded under that . . . eighteen-wheeler."

Declan's chest was heaving so hard I thought he might be having an asthma attack.

It hurt all over to watch how physically painful it was for him to say these words out loud, but I forced myself to sit there and listen.

"My mom . . . she . . . well, she left me twice, Scout. There's no other way to put it. That last time was for good. And I'm so mad at myself that when she died, when my mom died, I hadn't forgiven her for leaving us the first time. I had hated my mom, and then she died. I never got a chance to tell her I forgave her, to let her know how much I loved her. That was the worst thing."

The sound of our breathing filled the air. There was sadness floating in the air too, as though it were a physical thing that took up space and was composed of molecules.

"I'm so sorry, Dec."

He shrugged. "That's why you're lucky to still have your dad. Just to have him. Even if you're really mad at him or disappointed or whatever. You're lucky. Understand?"

I nodded.

"And he really might not have gone gambling, but even if he did, at least . . ." Declan's shoulders bobbed up and down. He swiped the back of his hand across his eyes.

I reached across the table and grabbed his other hand real gentle and let him cry, because sometimes all you could do was sit with someone and their hurt. And that hurt could be so strong it made you forget about your own worries.

Declan shook himself off and wiped his nose with a napkin. "I think you need to practice making crepes again, Scout."

"Huh?"

"I mean, if you want to be good at making them, you need to keep working at it. You can't just do it once and think you're a master crepe maker. Besides, I'm starving."

I got up and fished out one of Declan's old aprons. It was the one I'd worn at Halloween. "I totally agree." Threads of hope wound their way up my body and replaced the worried feelings inside me.

"You're definitely going to need to be able to make perfect crepes for when you live in Paris."

"Absolutely!" *Absolument!*

Once the ingredients were on the counter and we were ready to begin, Declan nodded. "And don't worry, Scout. I'll take good care of your Eiffel Tower money until you're ready to take it back."

I bumped my hip into Declan's. "I know you will."

And I did, with all my heart.

Dad was home when I got back to our trailer.

It was as though the argument had never happened, as though Dad had never stormed out.

He and Mom were sitting at the kitchen table together, playing Monopoly. From the piles of money in front of Mom, it looked like she was winning.

She was smiling.

So was he.

I heard music coming from our bedroom, so I knew Georgia was home.

Miss Genevieve looked up at me, then put his head onto his paws and let out a happy doggy sigh.

Maybe Dad hadn't gone to gamble at the dog park at all.

Maybe he'd just gone out for a walk . . . like Declan said. Or to a Gamblers Anonymous meeting.

I went over and hugged him hard around his neck. He held on to my arms and leaned into me.

It was so good to have him home.

To have everyone home.

It felt right.

Whole.

I was so sorry that Declan would never have that feeling again.

Unexpected News

MONDAY, FEBRUARY 22, WAS A really great day.
The air was chilly. The sun was shining.
A perfect winter day for Florida. I wished I could save this weather to have in the middle of summer.

At school I saw Declan and Todd in the hallways two different times each. They always waved or nodded or gave me a quick hug. It made me feel good. Even though I didn't have friends in my grade, I knew there were two people here who I could count on.

But the best thing of all happened at lunch.

Valerie Coombs, who used to sit at Jenna's table, came over with her bagged lunch and sat with me. Me!

We used to be friends in elementary school, before Jenna decided I must have cooties.

"Mind if I sit here?" she asked.

"Of course." I was grinning so hard it hurt. "I mean, of course not. Sit down."

Valerie sat and pulled an orange out of her bag.

"You can sit here anytime."

Valerie smiled. "Hey, do you still like all things Paris?"

Something inside me lit up. *"Oui. Oui."*

Valerie cracked up, and I felt better than I had at school in a long time.

On the walk home, I kept thinking about Valerie and what I might pack in my lunch to share with her tomorrow. I remembered she used to like baby carrots. I'd have to see if we had any at home. We even talked about going to the movies together in Winter Beach this weekend. I'd definitely dip into my Paris fund for that!

I planned to grab a quick snack at home, then walk Miss Genevieve and my other doggy customers. Things were definitely looking up.

But when I opened the door to our trailer, my plans for the rest of the afternoon disintegrated.

My sister was not supposed to be home. She should have been at work, scanning and bagging groceries at Weezie's Market and Flower Emporium. She was supposed to be earning money for the University of Vermont in the fall. She was definitely not supposed to be sitting at our kitchen table, staring off into space with rivers of tears rolling down her cheeks.

"Georgia?" I darted in and threw my backpack on the bench.

No response.

Miss Genevieve sat on the floor, pressed against the bench, with his head on her lap.

"Georgia!" I yelled to snap her out of her daze.

Miss Genevieve barked.

My sister still didn't move.

I got right in her face. "Is everything okay?"

"Nope," she whispered, fresh tears and snot running down her face.

I got her a strip of toilet paper to wipe her face, then sat across from her at the table.

Georgia's hair was all over the place. Her eyes were red and puffy. *Look at me, Georgia!* "What's wrong? You're scaring me. Did something happen to Mom?"

She shook her head.

"Dad?" *How terrible would it be if Dad finally got out of jail and something awful happened to him? What if he left us twice like Declan's mom?* My chest ached with the thought. "Georgia, did something happen to Dad?" I knew I was asking a question I didn't want the answer to.

She shook her head again, except this time tears dripped down onto the table. "I didn't get in."

"Huh?"

"Vermont." She let out a quivery breath. "I didn't get in."

"But how?"

She threw her hands up in the air. "Guess I suck."

"You . . ." I remembered Mom begging Georgia to apply to other colleges.

"Wait-listed, Cleveland. I was wait-listed."

"What does that even mean?" I wanted to do something to help my sister, but I wasn't sure what was happening.

Georgia wiped her leaking eyes on the toilet paper. "It means I'm not going to Vermont in the fall. It means I'm not going anywhere." She slumped into a heap of despair.

I wished Mom were here; she'd know what to say. Then I remembered something she did say. "Mom said you could always go to the community college." And for a moment I was happy, because this meant my sister wouldn't be leaving me. For a moment I was glad I'd have my sister in the bed next to mine for at least another year. This didn't seem like the worst news at all.

Georgia cried harder, and I felt terrible for being happy for even a second that she wouldn't be going away. I was the worst kind of sister. This was her one and only dream. "George, you'll figure something out. Hey, maybe it was a mistake. Maybe—"

"No mistake. I called."

"Oh."

Georgia got up and walked toward our room.

I was halfway off the bench and ready to follow her when she called without looking back, "Don't follow me."

All my good feelings about Valerie eating lunch with me evaporated.

I forced myself to walk Miss Genevieve and my other dogs, because even when someone's sister's dreams were destroyed and you felt horrible about it, dogs still needed to do their business.

An Answer

WHEN GEORGIA TOLD MOM AND Dad over our dinner of grilled cheese sandwiches and sliced apples, Dad responded with a glob of food inside his cheek. "That means you'll get to stay here at least another year!"

Mom and Georgia looked at him like he'd said the most awful thing ever, because he had.

"John?"

"What?" Dad swallowed and wiped his mouth on a napkin.

"This is all Georgia has ever wanted."

My sister started crying again.

Dad put his hands to his head. "I'm sorry, baby. I just

thought . . . it could make up for . . . some of the time I was . . . I'm . . . I . . . can't say anything right. I'm sorry."

Georgia cried louder.

Dad was up and out the door, half a sandwich and a pile of browning apple slices still on his plate.

Mom hugged Georgia, and they swayed back and forth. "Shh. He didn't mean it."

I wanted to hug them both.

I wanted someone to hug me.

It felt like my family was falling apart. *How did that happen so quickly?*

At lunchtime it seemed like the best day ever, but now . . .

I heard Miss Lola Lemon start and crunch across the gravel driveway, and my stomach plunged. I wanted to run out and beg him not to leave. But I wanted to stay with my sister and Mom, too.

My fingers automatically reached for the sides of my beret, and I tugged it more firmly on my head. Instead of it making me feel more secure, it felt heavy today. I wondered what it would feel like if I didn't wear the beret all the time. I had thought it brought me closer to Dad, especially when he was away, but maybe the beret was a bit of bad luck, sitting right there on top of my head. Jenna Finch broke her toe because of it, and it sure didn't help me keep my Paris Project money when Dad was heavy into gambling. And even though I wore it on the day of Dad's plea bargain, it didn't keep Dad out of jail. I was wearing it when Georgia found out she was wait-listed for Vermont, too. That dopey beret didn't do one good thing for me.

Maybe tomorrow I wouldn't wear it.

"Sweetheart," Mom said, "people who are wait-listed get in all the time. You just need to be patient."

"Mom, the only way for me to get in would mean other people declining their acceptances to Vermont. Who is going to decide not to go there?"

Mom continued to hold Georgia and rock her. "You'd be surprised, sweetheart. Kids could say no for all sorts of reasons. And that would open up a spot for you. Georgia, you definitely still have a chance to get in."

"I don't," Georgia wailed. "They didn't want me. After all my hard work. It didn't matter."

While Mom held Georgia and whispered soft words into her hair, I watched Miss Genevieve lying by the door and whimpering.

I wondered where Dad went.

Again.

• • •

That night Georgia fell asleep before I did.

I heard when Dad came home. And when he went into my parents' bedroom.

"Where were you, John?"

"Out."

"That's not gonna cut it."

Go, Mom!

Part of me was glad our walls were so thin I could hear everything. The other part of me didn't want to hear any of this. If Dad was gambling again, I didn't want to know. My heart couldn't take it.

"I'm frustrated, Glory. I want to work but can't get a job. I see how hard you're working every day, and it's killing me. Then I keep screwing things up around here. I didn't mean to make Georgia feel bad."

"John?"

"Hmm?"

"Where were you?"

A pause.

"I went to a Gamblers Anonymous meeting. It's where I went the other night too. I promised myself I'd never put you and the girls through that again."

"Oh, John."

I heard Mom crying, but I could tell it was because she was happy.

I was too.

Maybe I'd be able to ask Declan for my Eiffel Tower tin back.

Thank you, Dad.

A Happy Surprise

ONE EVENING IN LATE MARCH I came home from hanging out at Valerie's house in town. We listened to music and talked about school stuff, like how bad the lunchroom smelled that day because they were serving fish tacos. Blech! She even helped me look up French restaurants in Orlando on her laptop. We found one called Le Coq au Vin. It was *très* expensive, but a dish on their menu, Vegetable Strudel, looked so delicious I thought about spending some of my Paris Project money to take Declan, Todd, and Valerie there.

Spending time with Valerie made everything happening at home feel a little less awful; it also made me happy to know that one of Jenna's friends would rather hang out with me than with Jenna and her cool friends.

Mom and Georgia were at the table when I walked in. They were both grinning like crazy.

"What's going on?"

"You tell her," Georgia said.

Mom waved her hand. "It's your thing. *You* tell her."

Miss Genevieve came up and sniffed my sneakers. "Somebody tell her!" I yelled.

Mom scooted over on the bench and patted the seat beside her.

I raised my eyebrows at Georgia. When she nodded, I sat next to Mom.

Georgia laid her hands flat on the table. "Okay. You know your Paris Project list?"

"Of course."

"Well, Cleve, you're going to be able to cross a whole bunch of things off."

I felt a tingle of excitement, wondering if Georgia was going to treat for Le Coq au Vin. But I hadn't told her about it, so that couldn't be what she was talking about. I looked at Mom, hoping for a clue.

"I told your sister this was a bad idea," Mom blurted, but she was still grinning.

Georgia shook her head. "It's a great idea! The best idea I've ever had!"

"It's shortsighted," Mom said. "You've got to consider your future."

But Georgia looked so happy—the first time she'd displayed even a glimmer of joy since she learned she was wait-listed at the University of Vermont.

"We're going somewhere," Georgia said in a sneaky, mysterious way.

"Where?!" I shouted. Besides going to Winter Beach or the very occasional visit to see Aunt Allison and Ellen, I'd never been outside Sassafras. I realized Mom had been to only two special places outside Sassafras herself. We have magnets from both places on our fridge— Cleveland, Ohio, where she took a funny picture posing with a giant guitar outside the Rock & Roll Hall of Fame. (She and Dad went to Cleveland for my grandpop's funeral.) They couldn't afford to go into the Rock & Roll Hall of Fame, so they took a few pictures outside it. She and Dad also went to Atlanta, Georgia, on their honeymoon. They went to a Braves game, the Coca-Cola factory, and the aquarium. Mom said if she ever got a chance to go back, she'd want to visit the Center for Civil and Human Rights.

"Cleveland?" Georgia asked.

I couldn't sit still any longer. "Please tell me already!" I wondered if we'd won the lottery or maybe Dad finally got a job and this was how we were celebrating.

Georgia opened her laptop and turned the screen around so I could see it.

The most beautiful hotel I'd ever seen, the Enchanté Boutique Hotel, stared back at me. It looked like it came out of a fairy tale. A line below the photo read: *A French-style château where you will find a little bit of Paris in the heart of Silicon Valley.*

I turned the screen back toward my sister. I looked at Mom. Then at Georgia. They were both grinning like they'd just watched a thousand funny kitten and puppy videos online. My heart thundered. "What's going on?"

Georgia pulled her shoulders back. "We're going on a trip! I'm going to use the money I'd saved for Vermont for something good. Something important."

I swallowed hard. "What?"

"You, me, and Mom are going to the Enchanté."

"What about Dad?" It just popped out.

Mom put a hand on my shoulder. "We invited him, but he wants to stay here and keep looking for work. Your dad's pretty amazing, you know."

Georgia and I nodded.

"But he's adamant. Dad wants us to go on this trip,

thinks it's a great idea. He knows I've always wanted to travel, you've always loved Paris, and your sister has worked so hard that she deserves this. So, it would be a girls' trip. Just the three of us. I still don't think it's a wise move, but . . ."

Even though Mom sounded concerned, I could tell she was excited. All she had ever wanted was to do some traveling.

Georgia typed on her laptop, then pointed to the screen. "We'll be spending four days and three nights at the hotel. While we're there, we'll be dining at a French restaurant and going to a museum to see the French impressionists. It's all right in the same area."

Both Mom and Georgia were staring at me now.

"A French restaurant and the French impressionists?"

Georgia nodded.

"That hotel. It's so fancy."

She nodded again.

Then I realized something. "Does this mean we're going on a plane?!"

This time Mom nodded so hard her hair bounced all over the place. It looked like even her hair was happy.

I was so overwhelmed that I started blubbering.

Georgia hustled over and pushed in next to me. The three of us all mashed together on the bench seat—Georgia's arms around my shoulders and Mom's head leaning against mine.

"When?" I managed to say through my sobs.

"Last week in April." Georgia squeezed me tighter. "The plane and hotel are all booked. Mom tried to talk me into taking us to Epcot instead, but I knew that would feel fake. Plus, how would we see the French impressionists at Epcot? Am I right, Cleveland?"

"Oui. Oui." Although I thought Epcot could be really fun too. Jenna and her family went a couple of years ago, and she couldn't stop talking about how much fun she had visiting the different countries.

"Your sister looked into actually going to Paris," Mom said.

I sniffed. "You did?"

"Yup. I thought we could go over there and you could check out the school and all, but between the flights and passports and everything, it was just too expensive. This plan seemed like a good alternative."

"This plan sounds amazing," I said.

"Indeed." Mom nodded.

"It's going to be the best vacation ever!" Georgia screamed.

"Oh my . . ." I didn't think I'd ever been happier . . . while crying.

Georgia put her hand out. "All for one!"

Mom put her hand on top of Georgia's.

I put mine on top of Mom's.

"And one for all," Mom and I said at the same time.

It felt like Dad's hand needed to be on our pile, and I really wished he were coming on this trip, but I also knew how important it was to him to find a job. He'd been totally focused on it since he came home from jail nearly two months ago. Plus, he was going to the Gamblers Anonymous meetings a couple of evenings a week, too. And while he could probably go to them anywhere, Dad talked about how much he liked the people he had met at the meetings near us.

I looked at the picture of the hotel again on Georgia's computer. It was bathed in soft yellow light. I couldn't wait to see what it looked like in person!

A shiver ran down my spine. A French hotel. A French restaurant. And French art at a museum. This was incredible! *Incroyable!*

I would have tugged on the sides of my beret, but I hadn't been wearing it for four whole weeks now. I hadn't felt the need to.

A Third Chair

OVER THE NEXT FEW WEEKS Mom tried to talk Georgia out of spending all her savings on this trip, but she didn't try very hard. In fact, a week before we were supposed to go, on a Sunday—the day we used to devote to visiting Dad at the video visitation center—the three of us drove to Target in Winter Beach, and Georgia treated us all to new clothes.

I finally, finally got brand-new sneakers. They felt amazing. I hoped it took a long time before my toes poked holes through these.

Georgia and I pushed the red cart around the store together while Mom was in the greeting-card section, looking for a lovey-dovey card to sneak under Dad's pillow right before we left on the trip. It was nice to be in a place where people didn't give us the side-eye as we walked around the store, but even back home, people had seemed to stop judging us so much now that Dad was home. Things were getting better.

I nudged Georgia's arm. "You must have saved up a lot of money to go to Vermont."

She suddenly looked sad, and I felt horrible. "Yeah, Cleve. I did."

"Are you sure you want to spend it on this?"

After a deep breath, Georgia nodded. "I am. I definitely am."

"Okay then!"

She and I zoomed the red cart around Target, giggling and speaking French phrases to each other with exaggerated accents.

The people we passed looked at us like we were bonkers.

And I didn't care—*pas du tout!*

As soon as we got back from Target, I went right over to Declan's.

"You're going to have the best time," Dec said as we sat in the chairs outside his trailer. His dad had gotten rid of the old chairs and replaced them with comfortable new ones. But this time there were three chairs, not two.

"You will," Todd said. "The only time we ever went on vacation was a cruise with my grandparents, and I threw up the entire time."

Dec leaned over and punched Todd in the arm.

He rubbed his arm. "What? I did."

"I hope I don't throw up on the plane." I was scared to fly.

"You won't," Dec said. "It'll be the greatest thing ever. I wish we could go somewhere cool like that."

"Yeah," Todd said. "You're so lucky, Cleveland."

Lucky? I thought about how Dad spent seven months in jail. How Georgia didn't get into her dream school, even though she'd worked really hard. I thought about how hard Mom had been working, how many houses she had to clean every week. How lonely I felt sitting by myself in the lunchroom . . . until Valerie finally broke away from Jenna's group to sit with me. "At least now I'll check off more items on my Paris Project list, and then maybe I'll actually get to Paris."

"If you do," Dec said, "we might just have to go with you." He put his hand over his heart. "Because we couldn't survive without you, Scout."

"Yeah, you're stuck with us," Todd said to me before he shot a grin in Dec's direction.

"Hey," Dec said. "I can walk your dog customers while you're gone, if you need."

I sat forward. "Oh my gosh! I forgot. That would be great, Dec. Thanks so much. I'll let my customers know."

"I can help too," Todd said. "I love dogs."

"Of course you do," Dec said. "You also like rainbows and unicorns."

"And babies," I chimed in.

"And Santa Claus and the Tooth Fairy," Dec added.

Todd pushed him so hard Dec tumbled out of his chair. Then Todd laughed so hard he fell out of his own chair. They both lay on the ground, holding their stomachs from laughing so much.

When Dec ran into the trailer to use the bathroom, Todd cleared his throat. "Cleveland. I know I should have said this a while ago, but . . ."

I tilted my head.

"I wanted you to know I'm real glad your dad is back home. That's all."

I felt Todd's words seep into my heart. It had taken me some time to recognize that what happened wasn't his fault, and he'd been a good friend to me. "Thanks, Todd."

He nodded. We were both ready to move on.

Dec came out with strawberry ice pops.

I unwrapped mine and settled back in my chair, feeling the humid breeze, not quite believing I was having such a great time with Declan *and* Todd, but I was. They were such good friends.

I was lucky!

I also couldn't believe I'd be flying clear across the country to stay at a fancy French hotel with my mom and my sister. (Jenna Finch never got to do something amazing like that.)

Magnifique!

And We're Off!

D AD DROVE US TO THE gigantic Orlando airport in Miss Lola Lemon. He parked in front of our terminal, put on the hazard lights, and came around the car to help us with our suitcase. We decided to buy one suitcase for all our things because suitcases are expensive, plus you have to pay extra for them to fly on the plane with you.

"You ladies take care of each other. You're my whole world. You know that?"

Mom touched the tip of Dad's nose. "We'll be fine, John. You be good while we're gone."

"Glory, you do not have to worry about me. Roscoe

and I will be fine. And I promise I will have a job by the time you get home."

"John."

"I have a really good lead this time."

"Okay," she said, but I could tell Mom didn't believe him. He'd been close before but never got the job.

We all hugged Dad extra hard.

He patted the top of my beret. I'd decided to wear it again for the trip, and I think that made him happy. I was also wearing the black leggings and red-and-white-striped top I got at Christmas. It seemed like the perfect outfit for our very French trip. "Love you, Dad."

"You have fun now, Miss Cleveland. Enjoy every ever-loving French minute of this trip."

"I will, Daddy."

He gave Georgia a squeeze and lifted her off her feet, then set her down and looked right at her. "You're an amazing daughter and sister, Georgia. You know that. Right?"

She nodded. "Thanks, Dad. We'll bring you back something *très chic.*"

Mom got the biggest hug of all, and an embarrassingly long kiss.

"You all just have a wonderful time. Be safe."

He threw us kisses and waved as we walked into the chilly airport. I was sad Dad wasn't hopping on the plane with us, but glad Miss Genevieve wouldn't be home alone. I hoped Dad really did get a job. I knew how important it was to him and that it meant Mom wouldn't have to work as much.

Once we checked our suitcase, Mom grabbed hold of Georgia's hands and looked around the huge airport. "I can't believe we're getting out of Sassafras." She tapped her feet a bunch of times. "Oh, thank you, Georgia!"

My sister blushed. I think this one moment made it all worth it.

I felt like we were flying all the way to Paris, even though I knew we were really going to Los Altos, California.

It was an hour and a half until our flight boarded, so Georgia treated us to lunch at the Burger King in the terminal.

I knew this was going to be the most amazing trip ever!

The only way it could be any better was if Dad and Miss Genevieve had been able to come.

I stuffed five french fries into my mouth at the same

time, then chewed and swallowed their salty delicious-ness. "You're the best sister in the world."

Georgia shimmied her shoulders. "Tell me some-thing I don't know, Cleve."

And the three of us clinked our orange juice cartons together to toast our adventure.

The Best Day

THE AIR SMELLED GOOD WHEN we got off the plane. Fresh and clean and cool. While we rode the bumpy shuttle bus to our hotel, I noticed there were palm trees like in Sassafras. Maybe this part of the country wasn't so different after all.

We drove through neighborhoods with really big houses framed with pretty plants on neat tree-lined streets. It was gorgeous, so much nicer than Sassafras. And the whole drive to the hotel, I didn't see a single sign for someone selling worm tea!

The hotel was on a corner and looked like it did on the website. I may have gasped a little when we pulled up and the driver helped us out.

"This is how fancy people must live," I whispered to Mom.

She leaned down. "Today, Cleveland, we *are* fancy people."

Georgia grabbed my hand, and we strolled into the lobby like it was no big deal.

There was a woman behind a wooden desk. I had imagined she might be wearing a beret, but she wasn't.

"Welcome to the Enchanté."

While Georgia checked us in, I looked at a tiny replica of the Eiffel Tower on the desk. I shivered even though it wasn't cold, and remembered that my tin was still at Declan's house. I knew he was hiding it in the back of his underwear drawer, which was kind of gross, but pretty safe, because who would want to go in there? I'd ask him for it back after we got home. Dad had been doing great, and I'd have to learn to trust him at some point.

"Would you like someone to help you with your bags?" the woman asked.

Mom looked down at our single suitcase.

I wondered if she felt like we should have lots of suitcases—one for each of us.

"I've got it." I grabbed the suitcase. It wasn't even that heavy.

We decided to climb up the three sets of marble stairs, because Mom said they were so pretty. I wished I'd let them bring up the suitcase, because it got heavy by the second set of stairs, but that might have cost extra, and Georgia had already spent enough.

When Georgia opened the door to our hotel room, I forgot all about how heavy the suitcase had become.

Our room was amazing!

There was a big, comfy bed with a puffy white quilt on top. And another bed tucked against the wall. Framed paintings of gardens hung on the gold-striped wallpaper. And the best part: there was a fireplace!!! I'd never been anywhere with a fireplace before.

"Can I?"

"Go for it," Mom said.

So I flipped the switch and the fake logs at the bottom glowed orange. "Ooooh!"

Georgia and Mom went straight to the big bed with the fluffy white quilt. They flopped down, their hands behind their heads.

"This is the life," Mom said. "I could stay here the entire trip."

Georgia laughed. "It's so comfortable. You don't mind the little bed, do you, Cleve?"

I climbed onto the small bed. It didn't have a puffy

cover like theirs, but it had a soft gold blanket and a white sheet under that. "No, I love having my own private bed over here near the fireplace."

"It does look cozy," Mom said in a sleepy voice, dragging her body up into a standing position.

I leaped up and ran to the window and opened it with a crank. I looked down on the town of Los Altos. Everything was so shiny and new. While I loved the hotel room, I couldn't wait to get out there and walk around the cute shops with the colorful awnings. Maybe I wouldn't sleep during the whole trip so I could fit everything in.

"Mom, can I take a few photos with your phone to send Dad?"

"Of course, Cleveland. Make sure to get the fireplace and the big bed, too." She handed me her phone. "And tell him we love him."

"I will."

While I was taking a picture of the town, Mom suddenly yelled, "Look at this!"

Georgia and I crowded into the bathroom to admire the fancy soaps and square shampoo bottle Mom was holding. "Smell." She shoved a round soap wrapped in flowery paper under our noses.

"It smells better than any of the flowers at Weezie's

Market and Flower Emporium," Georgia said.

I took an extra-long sniff. "It smells like Paris."

After "freshening up," which entailed lying around, then washing our faces with thick white washcloths, we walked along every street in the little town and stopped in a tiny Parisian vintage clothing store. When we entered, the woman who worked there said, *"Bonjour!"* Between that and the frilly, lacy dresses, high heels with puffy pom-poms at the toe, and berets—tons of them in different colors—I felt like I was in a store in Paris. After that, we went to a coffee shop that used to be a train station. I told Georgia I wasn't thirsty, but she bought me a large *café au lait* anyway.

"It's the most French thing they have, Cleveland. You have to have it."

I really did.

Mom ordered a cup of mint tea, and she drank it with her pinkie out. I felt like we were finally sitting at a Parisian café, drinking our fancy drinks. *Oh, thank you, Georgia!*

My sister enjoyed a mug of steaming coffee and we shared a plate of madeleines. They're delicious French sponge-cake cookies that taste buttery and melt in your mouth. And are totally addictive. I felt like I'd been sucked into the world of the Madeline books.

Everything was so French, so perfect.

After enjoying our drinks and cookies, we walked some more around the town and discovered a beautiful bookstore. We spent a long, leisurely time in there, each of us meandering to the sections of the store we liked best. I used some of the spending money I'd brought to buy Declan a new cookbook; it had a whole section on fancy, fizzy drinks, so Dec could try concocting beverages other than limeade spritzers. I'd be happy to help him taste-test each and every one. The woman at the register wrapped it in paper with a bow for free! I knew Dec would love it.

Mom bought Dad a book about different kinds of cars.

"Perfect," Georgia and I said at almost the same time.

While the woman was wrapping Dad's gift, a girl entered the bookstore with a lady who must have been her grandma. The girl was wearing tights and a leotard, like she'd just come from ballet class. I smiled at her, and she gave me a shy wave in return. It seemed like a million years ago since I was at Miss Delilah's School of Dance and Fine Pottery, accidentally breaking Jenna Finch's pinkie toe.

Amazing how many things had changed since then.

Welcome Home!

I WAS SAD TO LEAVE THE beautiful French hotel. I looked
at it extra long before we shut the door so I'd remember all the details. I was sad to leave the museum where
the French impressionist paintings took my breath away.
They were more beautiful than I'd imagined. I was close
enough to touch them, even though there were guards
everywhere and that wasn't allowed. I was sad to leave the
French restaurant, where the bill was so high it made me
throw up a little in my mouth. But Georgia smiled when
she put the money in the black folder to pay our check,
and I knew she'd added a good tip for the server, like Dad
did that time we ate at Margaret Mitchell's Restaurant in
Winter Beach.

I was so sad to leave all of it behind . . . until we walked through the Orlando airport and there was Dad, waiting for us with the biggest smile I'd ever seen and his arms wide open.

"Welcome home, *mes amours!*"

"Dad, you learned French while we were gone," I said, surprised.

He laughed. "Just those two words. I thought they'd be the right ones to welcome you home."

We hugged and kissed him almost as much as when he came home from jail. Except now he wasn't so thin and was clean-shaven. I thought Dad looked happy because we were back home. But right there in the airport waiting area, he stood tall and made an announcement. "Potts family: I got a job!"

We hugged and kissed Dad all over again.

"You did it," I said.

"That's so great, Dad," Georgia added with a pat on his back. "Way to go."

Mom shook her head. "You continue to impress me, John Potts."

Dad hugged Mom, lifted her up, and twirled her in circles until she squealed for him to stop.

People were looking at us, but not in a mean and judgmental way. They looked happy. It was nice.

On the ride home, Dad explained that his old friend Dan Rousseau got him a job in parks and rec for Sassafras. He'd be responsible for keeping the parks and playgrounds clean and in good repair. "And the best part is I'll be outside all the time!"

It *was* the best part, because ever since Dad came home, he couldn't stand being cooped up indoors. He needed to be outside in the fresh, humid air.

"Now that I'll be working, Cleveland, I'm going to pay back every single dollar that I stole from you."

It was weird hearing Dad say it outright like that. But it was true. He had stolen from me.

I looked out at the twinkling stars in the dark night sky as we drove along. "Dad, you don't have to—"

"Every penny, Cleveland." Dad cleared his throat. "And I'm going to pay Ronnie Baker back too."

"Oh, John," Mom said.

I didn't think that part was such a good idea, so I chimed in from the backseat, "But, Dad, he sent you to jail. Why would you give him money?"

Even though Dad was driving, he reached a hand into the backseat.

I met his fingers, and he squeezed. "Baby girl, Mr. Baker did the right thing. And it was the best thing he could have done for me."

"Going to jail was the best thing?" I folded my arms across my chest. I wondered if Dad had gotten so happy about his new job that it had made him a little confused.

"Yes," Dad said. "If he hadn't pressed charges after the third time I stole from him, I would've kept right on doing what I was doing."

"Three times?" Georgia said.

"Yup. He let me slide the first two times. Like I said, going to jail was the best thing for me."

Mr. Baker knew Dad stole from him twice and let it go? I don't know if I would've done that. I felt bad for the awful things I'd thought about Mr. Baker.

"But you're glad you went to jail?" Georgia asked.

"Look, I wasn't glad to be away from all of you, but the truth is, if I hadn't gone to jail, I'd probably still be stealing to gamble."

Mom reached over and squeezed Dad's shoulder.

"It's an ugly truth," Dad said. "But it is the truth. Now I'm going to try and mend all the relationships I've broken and return every dollar I took."

I felt choked up, hearing Dad say those words. Part of me had wanted to hear them for a long time. It was such a relief, like one last missing puzzle piece snapped satisfyingly into place.

We were quiet for a while, until he asked us about

our trip, and then none of us could shut up for a minute about how awesome it was.

Because it was!

The Paris Project
By Cleveland Rosebud Potts

~~1. Take ballet lessons at Miss Delilah's~~
~~School of Dance and Fine Pottery (to~~
~~acquire some culture).~~
Ballet is not the answer . . . no matter what the question is!
√ 2. Learn to cook at least one French
dish and eat at a French restaurant (to be
prepared for the real thing). *Crepes—savory
and sweet! Délicieuses!*
*My favorite part of the French restaurant
was the cute server who was totally flirting
with Georgia the whole time.*
√ 3. Take in paintings by the French
impressionists, like Claude Monet's *Water-
Lily Pond*, at an art museum so I can
experience what good French art is (more
culture!).
√ 4. Continue learning to speak French

(will come in handy when moving to France
and needing to find important places, like
la salle de bains, so I can go *oui oui*—ha-ha!—
French bathroom humor).
5. Apply to the American School of Paris
(must earn full scholarship to attend for
eighth grade. You can do this, Cleveland!).
6. Move to France! *(Fini!)*
Good riddance, Sassafras, Florida!

C'est la Vie!

MAY PASSED IN A BLUR.

School was winding down. If I wasn't walking dogs after school, I was hanging out with Valerie or with Dec and Todd.

I even told Jenna Finch off.

I was in the lunch line to buy ice cream again, and there she was right behind me. "Oh look," Jenna said. "You actually have enough money to *buy* something for a change." Instead of shying away, I whirled around and faced her. It took all my restraint not to stomp on her formerly injured pinkie toe. "Jenna Finch"—I pulled my shoulders back—"I am just as good as you are, so keep your snooty opinions to yourself."

And she did.

Jenna's mouth formed an O of complete and utter surprise; then she closed it and cast her gaze downward.

I knew that look.

Jenna Finch was ashamed.

Things were going well on the home front, too.

Dad came home sweaty and happy from work every day and still went to Gamblers Anonymous meetings a couple of nights a week.

He started paying me back, and I put every dollar into the Eiffel Tower tin at Declan's. It's a good thing it was a large tin, because that thing was really filling up! I decided to leave it at Declan's house a little bit longer. Just to be extra safe. Then I'd probably have to open a bank account, because it was a lot of money.

Mom was able to give up some of her cleaning jobs, so she didn't look so tired and she was around more often. She even started making dinner again, so Georgia didn't have to do it all the time.

Georgia had decided to go to the community college in the fall and didn't seem so miserable about it. She also put up about a thousand pictures of mountains and people skiing and other Vermont-looking things on the walls in our bedroom. She cut the pictures out from Mom's travel magazines. Mom didn't spend quite so much time looking through them these days.

"I'm going to get there someday," Georgia said, looking at all the pictures on our walls.

"Maybe next year," I offered helpfully.

Georgia nodded. "Maybe." Then she looked at me. "Hey, do you want to put up some pictures of Paris, Cleve? I could help you find them in Mom's magazines."

I shook my head. "Your pictures are good, George. They make me feel cooler, which is a welcome change."

"Well then, you have a good imagination." Georgia waved a book in front of her face, but I knew it wasn't doing anything to dissipate the heat in our trailer. We were heading toward another hotter-than-hot summer, and there wasn't much anyone could do about it.

Miss Genevieve didn't seem to mind the heat. He napped and snored and was his usual happy self.

Everything was going fine in the Potts home until one day I was in bed looking through an old copy of *Madeline* I'd borrowed from the Sassafras Public Library, when Georgia let out the world's loudest scream.

My foot tangled in my sheet as I rocketed up.

Outside my room, I bumped into Mom and Dad.

Miss Genevieve was underfoot, barking.

"What?" Mom shrieked as we ran. "Are you hurt?"

Georgia screamed again. And again. "Oh my gosh!!!"

Dad got to the kitchen table first.

Mom and I crowded around him.

Georgia was staring at her computer with one hand over her mouth. She was shaking her head.

"What, George?" Mom asked, trying to get a look at her screen. "What's wrong?"

"Tell us," Dad said.

"Yeah, Georgia." I moved closer.

Tears leaked from Georgia's eyes. "I got in." She lowered her hand.

"What?" Mom shook her head.

"The University of Vermont." Georgia blinked, blinked, blinked. "I got accepted."

"I thought you were wait-listed," I said.

"I was." Georgia put her hand over her mouth again, then dropped it. "I guess enough people declined."

"Why would anyone do that?" I asked.

Georgia shrugged. "When I called, they said I was near the top of the waiting list, but I thought . . . I thought they were giving me a line, you know."

Mom squeezed in next to Georgia and looked at the screen.

Dad ran a hand through his hair. "Well, this is great news, George."

But I could tell by Dad's eyes that he was a little sad. This meant Georgia would be leaving us in about three months.

I felt it in my gut too, but I knew how much this meant to my sister. "Yeah," I said. "Great news, George!"

She shook her head and let out a laugh that might have been a cry. "No. No, it's not."

"What? Why not?" Mom asked.

My sister shook her head.

"George?" Mom prodded.

"I can't go." Tears spilled down my sister's cheeks. "I spent almost all my money on our trip."

"Didn't you get scholarships?" Dad asked. "Mom told me you were applying for lots of them."

"Yes. The school part is almost entirely paid for, but I don't have the money to fly up there or buy books or for the fees or anything else. I spent the bulk of it on our vacation." Then my sister started laughing, really laughing, but not in a funny way. In a way that scared me. "I actually got in and now I can't go."

I looked at Mom and Dad, hoping they'd have a solution, some money they'd secretly stashed away somewhere, a long-lost relative who'd died and left us loads of cash. But my parents didn't have answers; they had worry lines on their foreheads.

It took me about two seconds to make up my mind. "You're going!"

"Cleveland?" Mom said cautiously.

"Wait here."

I ran the whole way, past the pool and car-wash station, until I could see the trailer plastered in bumper stickers with the three chairs out front.

Dec opened the door while I was still knocking. "What's up, Scout?"

"I need the tin."

"Huh?"

"The Eiffel Tower tin, Dec. I need it right now."

"Is everything okay?"

I looked at my best friend. At his red hair and matching freckles. At his pointy ears. At his kind, concerned eyes. "Yes, Declan. Everything will be okay once you give me the tin."

He hurried to his room and came back with it.

"Thanks. I promise I'll explain everything soon."

"Okay, Scout."

I ran all the way home, thinking about how much cash there was inside the metal box clutched to my chest. Earning ninety dollars a week added up fast, especially over all those months. I'd saved $3,280, plus Dad had paid me back $250 so far.

Miss Genevieve licked my ankle when I came in, but I didn't have time to pet him.

Mom and Dad were sitting opposite Georgia at the kitchen table now. I could tell she'd still been crying.

"I want you . . . to have it." I bent forward, gasping for air, holding out the tin to her. "All of it, except . . . I need about three hundred dollars . . . to buy Declan a KitchenAid mixer . . . he's been wanting . . . forever. But the rest . . . is yours."

Georgia smiled. "That's real nice, Cleveland."

I put the Eiffel Tower tin into my sister's hands.

"But I can't take your Paris money."

I squeezed in next to my sister, our legs pressed up against each other's. "Oh, yes you can. I don't need Paris. You gave me Paris in Los Altos. That was the best time I've ever had in my life." I looked at Mom and Dad, who were holding hands on the table. I glanced at Miss Genevieve, snorfling away in his favorite sleeping position on the floor. I thought of Valerie. I thought of Declan and Todd. "I have everything I need right here. Paris will be there when I'm older. I want you to take the money. There's enough to fly you up there, buy a bunch of books, pay fees, plus more. I want you to have it, George. I want you to go to Vermont . . . even though I'm going to miss you like nobody's business."

"Oh, Cleve." Georgia turned and hugged me so hard that I reached up to keep my beret from falling off, completely forgetting that I'd stopped wearing it again after our trip.

Georgia held the tin tightly and kissed me on the cheek. "You'll visit me in Vermont."

"You know it."

Mom sniffed.

Dad smiled.

Miss Genevieve did what he did best—let out a startling snore.

We all laughed.

Then Georgia messed up my hair and leaned her head against mine. "Cleveland Rosebud Potts, *you're* the best sister."

I shrugged. "Tell me something I don't know."

C'est la vie!

The Paris Project
By Cleveland Rosebud Potts

~~1. Take ballet lessons at Miss Delilah's School of Dance and Fine Pottery (to acquire some culture).~~

Ballet is not the answer . . . no matter what the question is!

✓ 2. Learn to cook at least one French dish and eat at a French restaurant (to be prepared for the real thing). *Crepes—savory and sweet! Délicieuses!*

My favorite part of the French restaurant was the cute server who was totally flirting with Georgia the whole time.

✓ 3. Take in paintings by the French impressionists, like Claude Monet's *Water-Lily Pond*, at an art museum so I can experience what good French art is (more culture!).

✓ 4. Continue learning to speak French (will come in handy when moving to France and needing to find important places, like *la salle de bains,* so I can go *oui oui*—ha-ha!— French bathroom humor).

5. Apply to the American School of Paris (must earn full scholarship to attend for eighth grade. You can do this, Cleveland!).

6. Move to France! *(Fini!)*

Good riddance, Sassafras, Florida!

Paris can wait!

Acknowledgments

Public libraries are our treasure troves of thought, wisdom, information, and imagination. Libraries open doors, open minds, and offer access to the wider world no matter who you are or where you live. Librarians hold the sacred task of guiding their patrons' travels and providing passports to those wider worlds. I'm filled with gratitude for the public libraries and librarians who have saved me and shaped me, beginning with the Northeast Regional branch of the Free Library of Philadelphia. Libraries, to me, always feel like home.

Investing in public education and our children means investing in our future. I'm brimming with gratitude for educators who teach young people to embrace the wider world and think critically. Special thanks to those who share their passion for reading and writing to give young people tools for a better life and a way to share their experiences, feelings, and voices. You're creating ripples that impact the universe.

I'd like to thank my agent, Tina Dubois, who holds my career in her capable hands with a wise head and kind heart.

My editor, Krista Vitola, renewed my zest and passion

for this work I love with her energy and dedication.

Because every book is a collaborative effort, I appreciate the talented team of dedicated individuals at Simon & Schuster Books for Young Readers for working tirelessly to create great books to share with the world. It's a delight to be part of this grand team!

My family and friends have lifted me up and continue to fill me with gratitude and grace every day of this wild and wonderful ride.

Always and forever, my deepest and abiding love to Andrew, Jake, and Dan—my heartbeats.

French Words and Phrases Used in This Book

absolument—absolutely

bonjour—hello

café au lait—coffee with milk

Ce n'était pas bon.—This was not good.

Ce n'était pas juste.—This wasn't fair.

C'est la vie.—That's life.

cordialement—cordially

délicieuses—delicious

difficile—difficult

enchanté—enchanted

fini—finished

formidable—wonderful

gros problème—big problem

humiliant—humiliating

imbécile—idiot

incroyable—incredible

J'ai des problèmes.—I have problems.

Je suis irritée.—I am irritated. (if it's a girl speaking)

la salle de bains—the bathroom

l'espoir—hope

magnifique—magnificent

merveilleux—wonderful

mes amours—my loves

Mieux vaut prévenir que guérir.—Better safe than sorry.

mon ami—my friend (a male friend)

mon amie—my friend (a female friend)

oh, beau chien—oh, beautiful dog

Oh la la la la!—Oh no no no no!

oui—yes

parfait—perfect

pas du tout—not at all

pas question—no way

tellement gros—so big

terrible—terrible

très—very

très bien—very good

très cher—very expensive

très chic—very stylish

très gênant—very embarrassing

très importants—very important

un étreinte—a hug

un millier de fois—a thousand times

zut—heck

Recipe for Declan's Limeade Spritzer

You will need:

- 1 tablespoon agave (or another sweetener)
- juice from half a lime (or 1 tablespoon bottled lime juice)
- 4 ounces cold water
- 4 ounces seltzer
- a few mint leaves (optional)

Instructions:

In a tall glass, pour in agave (or other sweetener). Add the lime juice. Add cold water and seltzer. Stir. Top with mint leaves if you like. Enjoy!

Information/Statistics about Parental Incarceration in the United States of America

Ten million children across the USA have had a parent incarcerated at some point in their lives.[1]

More than 2.7 million children have a parent behind bars.[2]

One in nine black children have a parent in prison.[3]

One in twenty-eight Latinx children have a parent in prison.[4]

One in fifty-seven white children have a parent in prison.[5]

Eighty percent of women in jail are mothers.[6]

Visits and phone calls are an economic burden shouldered by the family, as is the hardship of traveling far from home to visit a loved one.[7]

One in fourteen children in the USA have experienced the incarceration of a loved one.[8]

Loved ones of the incarcerated are routinely ignored, neglected, stigmatized, and endangered.[9]

1. National Resource Center on Children and Families of the Incarcerated, *Children and Families of the Incarcerated Fact Sheet* (Camden, New Jersey: Rutgers University, 2014), https://nrccfi.camden.rutgers.edu/files/nrccfi-fact-sheet-2014.pdf.

2. National Resource Center on Children and Families of the Incarcerated.

3. National Resource Center on Children and Families of the Incarcerated.

4. National Resource Center on Children and Families of the Incarcerated.

5. National Resource Center on Children and Families of the Incarcerated.

6. Elizabeth Swavola, Kristine Riley, and Ram Subramanian, *Overlooked: Women and Jails in an Era of Reform* (New York: Vera Institute of Justice, 2016), https://www.vera.org/publications/overlooked-women-and-jails -report.

7. Stacey M. Bouchet, *Children and Families with Incarcerated Parents: Exploring development in the field and opportunities for growth* (Baltimore, MD: Annie E. Casey Foundation, January 2008), http://www.aecf.org /m/resourcedoc/AECF-ChildrenandFamilieswithIncarceratedParents -2008.pdf#page=4.

8. Nash Jenkins, "1 in 14 U.S. Children Has Had a Parent in Prison, Says New Study," *Time*, October 27, 2015, http://time.com/4088385 /child-trends-incarceration-study/.

9. POPS the Club (website), accessed June 11, 2019, https:// popsclubs.org.

Children of Incarcerated Parents Bill of Rights
(www.sfcipp.org)

I have the right . . .

1. to be kept safe and informed at the time of my parent's arrest.

2. to be heard when decisions are made about me.

3. to be considered when decisions are made about my parent.

4. to be well cared for in my parent's absence.

5. to speak with, see, and touch my parent.

6. to receive support as I face my parent's incarceration.

7. not to be judged, blamed, or labeled.

8. to have a lifelong relationship with my parent.